Readers love The Underground Club series by SJD PETERSON

Override

"I loved this story. Little angst, no anger issues, no overblown drama, just two men finding a way to meet in the middle and merge their worlds."

—Alpha Book Club

"The strength of *Override* is definitely the strong and steady connection between Seth and Donavan and their growing romance."

—Sinfully: Gay Romance Book Reviews

"…I like my stories with a good build-up, well portrayed characters, good chemistry, and bare minimum angst. This is exactly what I got here and I read it in one sitting, enjoying every page."

—Three Books Over the Rainbow

Limitless

"SJD Peterson def has a way of sucking in the readers. This book is the perfect example of that."

—Gay Book Reviews

"I recommend this to everyone who's intrigued with BDSM, the Dom/sub relationship, the concept of pain mixed with pleasure, and flawed, realistic men who more than deserve a happy ending."

—Long and Short Reviews

By SJD PETERSON

BAMF
Going Off Grid
Innocence to the Max
Leon
Masters & Boyd
My Hometown
A Night Never Forgotten
Plan B
Remember When
Rival Within
Roger
Romance Redefined
With S.A. McAuley: Ruin Porn
Splintered (Audio Only)
Something's Brewing at Joe's
Tuck & Cover

BEYOND DUTY
Beyond Duty
Mauled

GUARDS OF FOLSOM
Riveted
Pup
Tag Team
Pony
Roped
Mauled
Bound

WHISPERING PINES
RANCH
Lorcan's Desire
Quinn's Need
Ty's Obsession
Conner's Courage
Jess's Journey
Riveted

THE UNDERGROUND
CLUB
Override
Limitless
The Edge

Published by DREAMSPINNER PRESS
www.dreamspinnerpress.com

THE EDGE

SJD PETERSON

Published by

DREAMSPINNER PRESS

5032 Capital Circle SW, Suite 2, PMB# 279, Tallahassee, FL 32305-7886 USA
www.dreamspinnerpress.com

The Edge
© 2018 SJD Peterson.

Cover Art
© 2018 Ronaldo Gutierrez, Photographer
Cover Design
© 2018 Paul Richmond
Cover content is for illustrative purposes only and any person depicted on the cover is a model.

Trade Paperback ISBN: 978-1-64080-173-8
Digital ISBN: 978-1-64080-174-5
Mass Market Paperback ISBN: 978-1-64108-074-3
Library of Congress Control Number: 2017917048
Trade Paperback published July 2018
v. 1.0

Printed in the United States of America
∞
This paper meets the requirements of
ANSI/NISO Z39.48-1992 (Permanence of Paper).

To all those who went to the edge and came back whole and healed.

Prologue

JOSHUA STOOD in the center of his room, his flesh still warm and damp from his recent shower. Tonight, Nash would be taking him to the club for the first time since the night Nash brought him home. It had only been a couple of days since they'd recommitted to their contract, and Joshua was still trying to get used to his schedule and rules. He'd much rather stay home. He didn't want to embarrass Nash. But Nash wanted to go, and Joshua wouldn't deny him. He was both nervous and excited. It meant a lot to him that Nash wanted to show him off, and yeah, there was a part of him that wanted to throw it in the face of every person who turned up their nose at him, gave him looks of pity or—especially—nasty sneers, like he got from folks like Troy. He would be kneeling at the feet of the most attractive Dom in the place. *My Dom.* The thought made him smile.

"That's a good look on you," Nash commented as he stepped up close to Joshua.

"Naked?"

"No… well yes, but I was talking about the smile," Nash clarified. "Care to share what you were thinking about that caused it?"

"You, Sir," Joshua said with absolute conviction. The smile he got in return curled Joshua's toes. It looked damn fine on Nash's face too.

"Suck-up." Nash sniffed.

"Only stating facts, Sir."

"All right, let's get you dressed before Malcolm scolds me for being late." Nash cocked his head, a mischievous glint in his eyes. "Although, he may forgive me if he learns it was because I had you bent over with my…." He shook his head and pointed a finger at Joshua. "Stop tempting me."

Joshua clamped his lips to keep back the snort of laughter that threatened.

Nash walked over to the chair and picked up a pair of leather pants, went to his knees in front of Joshua, and held them out for Joshua to step into. A thrill raced through him at seeing his master on his knees before him, and his dick twitched.

Nash must have read Joshua's thoughts because he pointed at him again. "Don't get any ideas, boy. Come is a bitch to get out of leather."

"Only if you spill a drop, Sir."

"Cheeky sub."

Unfortunately, Nash didn't try to prove Joshua right. Instead, he slid the pants up Joshua's thighs. Joshua sighed as the soft leather caressed his skin and then moaned wantonly when Nash took Joshua's hard dick in hand and adjusted it within the leather.

Once Joshua was dressed, Nash rolled to his feet and retrieved the black T-shirt from the chair. After he helped Joshua into it, Joshua caught a glance of his reflection in the mirror and pushed his chest out a little more, preening.

I look fabulous, darling. Joshua rolled his eyes at his silliness. This was a serious night, one in which he needed to focus, not joke around.

Wide wristbands and black leather boots with heavy soles completed the look. They fit perfectly, as did the rest of his clothes—they looked and felt good. Nash stepped back, crossed his arms, and ran a critical eye up and down Joshua's body, a frown marring his brow. Suddenly, he snapped his fingers and went to the armoire, threw open the doors, and started rummaging through its contents.

Joshua's eyes went wide when he saw what was in Nash's hand. He couldn't help but jerk when Nash stepped up behind him and slid the collar around his neck, making sure the small O-ring was in the divot of his throat. He hadn't worn a collar in a long time and had mixed feelings about it being around his neck. The last time he had one on had been during a dark period of his life, and removing it had been the darkest. Nash buckled it into place, the collar tightening briefly. A strange sound escaped Joshua's lips and his pulse instantly kicked up.

"Too tight."

It wasn't tight, in no way restricting his ability to breathe or swallow, but it felt like a huge weight pushing down on him, and with it came unwanted memories.

Nash wrapped his arms around Joshua, resting his chin on Joshua's shoulder. "Hey, you're shaking. You okay?"

Joshua blinked to dispel the images of another place, another time, another collar. He swallowed his unease and nodded. "I'm okay, Sir."

Nash ran a soothing hand over Joshua's belly, up his chest to the collar. "Don't let this distress you. It's simply for show. We have a lot of work to do together before we can talk about your actual collar."

"I know, but…." Joshua's voice cracked. The idea of being collared by anyone, even Nash, wasn't comforting—it was scary as hell. Collars equaled ownership, possession, humiliation, betrayal, disappointment…. The trembling increased, and he struggled to take a full breath.

A gentle hand landed on his shoulder, stroking, comforting. "Look at me."

Panic spread through Joshua. *Run!* His heart rate kicked up, sweat trickled down his temples.

"Look at me. Focus. Right here," Nash encouraged.

Joshua lifted his eyes and met Nash's concern-filled gaze.

"That's it. Right here. Long deep breaths."

Joshua focused on Nash, on his soothing touch. It took several minutes, but eventually he pushed the unwanted memories away, stood in the here and now. He took a deep, full breath and blew it out deliberately, the trembling easing.

"That's it. Would you like me to remove the collar?" Nash offered.

Just for show. Joshua took another deep breath. "No, I'm okay, Sir."

"Are you sure? Would you like to stay home and talk about what just happened?"

Joshua shook his head. "No, Sir. I'm looking forward to going." And he was. He concentrated on Nash, the club, his pride in being at Nash's side. He took the white room, the battered collar, the look of disdain, all the negative images the collar had invoked and shoved them into his mental safe, secured the lock. He was good at hiding things, even from himself. He took another long breath and let it out.

Nash pressed a gentle kiss to Joshua's temple. "All right. Let's go have some fun and enjoy each other. But we will be talking about this later. Understood?"

Joshua nodded. "Yes, Sir." He had no plan to keep the agreement. Those things, the past, had no business being part of his future. Eventually, they would fade into forgotten memories. At least he hoped.

Nash kissed him one last time before releasing him. He then walked around Joshua and stood a few feet away, facing him. "You, my boy, are pure perfection."

Joshua focused on the compliment, let it take over his thoughts until he could feel it swelling his chest, the pride coursing through him. He squared his shoulders and adjusted his stance. "Thank you, Sir."

"I'm going to be the most envied Dom in the place tonight, and I can't wait to show you off."

"I hope I don't disappoint you, Sir."

Nash shook his head. "You never could. All right, let's go make the members of the Underground weep with envy."

Joshua followed Nash out of the room. He didn't know whether they would weep, but Joshua certainly was going to do his best to make sure they envied Nash by being the perfect sub. Nash deserved nothing less.

From the moment Joshua followed Nash into the Underground Club, it felt like every eye was on him. He didn't dare lift his head, but his skin prickled as their gazes bore into him. Out of his peripheral vision, he saw club members, subs and Doms alike, with looks of disgust on their faces as he and Nash passed. Others appeared shocked, indifferent, or unimpressed. Joshua did his best to keep his posture while walking to heel. The reaction to his presence made it hard to breathe, let alone walk with any kind of pride. He was a fucking poser, a loser, and he didn't belong here. Not with Nash. Not with anyone.

Malcolm was sitting at the bar, but as soon as they approached, he stood and gestured for Nash to follow him. Malcolm stopped at the open door to the back dining room and held out his arm. "I thought we'd dine in private. We have so much to catch up on. We can enjoy the crowds after."

Nash pecked Malcolm's cheek as he passed. "You simply want to gossip without others overhearing."

"Yes, well, that too," Malcolm said. He raked his gaze up and down Joshua.

Joshua held his breath, worried what he would see when Malcolm looked back up. Joshua was spared when Nash took the seat opposite Malcolm. Joshua went instantly to his knees, adjusted his posture, held his head high, and eyes lowered. He couldn't look at Malcolm, didn't even attempt to. He couldn't stand to see the same look of disdain the others had worn. He was having a hard enough time not running. Seeing disgust in Malcolm's eyes would shred the last of Joshua's restraint.

Nash ran his fingers through Joshua's hair, but it did nothing to help him relax. Nash wanted him here, wanted to show him off, but Joshua was seriously questioning Nash's decision.

"Chardonnay, boy," Malcolm said.

Joshua got a glimpse of Conrad, who said, "Yes, Sir," before he scurried off.

"When are you going to take that boy under your wing? The way he looks at you, the poor thing is in need of your skilled hand," Nash said.

"He's much too young for me," Malcolm responded. "Your boy, on the other hand, seems to be flourishing."

Joshua stiffened. His pulse raced, and the sound of blood rushing in his ears made it difficult to hear. Had Malcolm actually complimented him?

"That he is," Nash replied. It sounded like he might even have a hint of pride in his voice, but again, the noise in Joshua's head was making it difficult to be sure. Maybe he only heard what he wanted to hear. Nash had to have witnessed the way others reacted to their entrance. No way could Nash be proud of Joshua.

The prickling sensation he'd experienced when walking into the club intensified, and Joshua tuned out Nash and Malcolm and concentrated on slowing his racing heart. He clamped down on his trembling muscles, taking deep breaths in through his nose and releasing them slowly. Dammit, if he didn't get the rush of sound out of his head and get control over his body, he was going to lose it.

Conrad returned to the table with a bottle of wine, and while he filled the glasses, Nash leaned down and whispered in Joshua's ear.

Joshua heard "Go with Conrad," and although Nash was still talking, he tuned it out. He couldn't concentrate on what was being said as it took everything he had not to jump up and run in his excitement to get away from Nash and have a few minutes to collect himself.

He forced himself to remain on his knees, his posture erect, and said, "Yes, Sir." He rolled to his feet, locked down on his trembling legs, and curled his hands into fists behind his back to hide the way they shook.

Nash sat back in his chair. Joshua held his breath, doing his best not to give away how close he was to losing it. He knew better than to look up, and it took every bit of pure willpower not to break into a run.

"Conrad, could you escort Joshua to the bar and assure no one steals my boy away?" Nash finally asked.

"It would be my pleasure, Sir."

Joshua kept his steps slow and measured as he followed Conrad, but it was with great difficulty. It was as if someone had attached a vise around his lungs and was steadily tightening it. He dug his fingernails into his palms, the spark of pain as he penetrated his flesh giving him enough focus to keep his composure. The instant Joshua stepped out of the private dining area, he lowered his head and rushed to the bathroom. He cared nothing about his posture or etiquette or what people thought; he had to get the hell out of there. It would be a harder hit to Nash's reputation if his boy had a panic attack and freaked out in the middle of the club.

Inside the bathroom, Joshua locked the door with a trembling hand then turned and slid down the door. He grabbed the back of his head with both hands, fisted his fingers in his hair, and pulled his head down, rolling into a semiball.

He didn't belong here; every set of eyes that settled on him with disgust was proof of that. Nash was a decent guy. Surely he thought he was doing the right thing by bringing him here tonight. Nash was wrong. He was so very wrong.

Since his meltdown, when Joshua nearly picked up that knife and put it to his flesh, he'd been questioning everything, especially his decision to be with Nash Mead. An epic battle raged within Joshua, desire versus need, right versus. wrong, worth versus. insignificance. Tonight need, wrong, and insignificance were the clear front-runners.

NASH SIPPED at his wine until Joshua and Conrad left. "Okay, I can tell by the way you're vibrating that you're dying to ask me something. Go ahead."

"Joshua looks amazing, but how are his sessions with Cedric going?"

Nash shrugged. "He's only had two visits and is very tight-lipped about what he and Cedric talk about. It's driving me nuts, as you can imagine, but I have to respect his privacy in this."

Malcolm nodded. "I'm sure it's very difficult, but you're doing the right thing. He will come to you in time when he is ready."

"I hope so."

"There you go, doubting me again." Malcolm sniffed, then softened it with a curious smile. "And his pain issues?"

"The cock cage is still working quite well, but I fear he is beginning to get used to it. He no longer groans or complains—he's quite eager to have it on, in fact."

"Yes, then you must change it up."

"I know." Nash nodded. "Another thing I'm going to have to approach is his collar."

Malcolm's eyes went wide. "You think that's wise?"

Nash pursed his lips. "Give me a little credit. He is nowhere near ready to be collared. I was referring to his reaction to wearing one tonight. He started to panic when I put one on him. I was able to get him to focus on me and we worked through it, but whatever the reason behind the reaction, it has left him shaken."

"Did you ask him about it?"

"Of course, but he wasn't ready to discuss it. Trust me. We will be addressing it, and soon."

"The poor boy." Malcolm sighed. "I hope you are able to bring him peace soon."

"Honestly, Malcolm, I don't know if the boy will ever have it. His past is always lurking just below the surface."

"I must disagree. I think if anyone can help the boy find it, it is you. That he's willing to see a professional to deal with the hardships bestowed upon him while growing up and throughout his young life speaks volumes for what he is willing to do for you."

"I don't want him to do it for me—"

Malcolm held up his hand. "There is nothing wrong with him going into counseling to please you or doing it for you. You're his strength, his motivation, and in time, he'll do it for himself as well."

Nash stared at the far wall, unblinking, thinking. Malcolm was probably right. In fact, it was highly probable, and what did it matter who Joshua was doing it for as long as he was getting the help he needed? That's what mattered most.

Nash met Malcolm's gaze. "I hadn't thought of it that way."

"It's a good thing you have me to remind you," Malcolm said smugly. "So, what's next on your to-do list?"

"To be everything he needs."

"What about your needs?"

"Right now, I'm focusing on his."

Malcolm gave Nash a disapproving look. "In order for your relationship to work, both of your needs must be met."

"I know, but honestly, I am trying, and I believe Joshua is as well." The truth of it settled into Nash. "Joshua may not be whole at the moment, but every day he learns and grows and heals. My need is to teach him and complete him, which makes me whole as well."

"Going to be one hell of a rocky road, my friend."

Nash smiled broadly. "The road to happiness usually is."

Malcolm held up his glass. "Here's to a successful journey."

Nash clinked his glass against Malcolm's before taking a sip. It wasn't going to be easy, but Nash was committed. Joshua's healing was Nash's definition of success.

~*~

My shrink has suggested I start keeping a journal to write down my feelings each night. Therapy, he calls it. Help me get in touch with my feelings, he tells me. Well, I'm sure he's making me do this because he'll want to talk about what I wrote, so I'm going on record as saying I think this is a really, really, really stupid idea. I'm writing to myself for fuck's sake. If that isn't stupid, I don't know what is. I will be the good little boy and play along.

So, my feelings huh?

Well, beyond feeling like a fool, I'm also irritated. I woke up in a piss-poor mood, and as I'm sitting here in my bed with Nash in his across the hall, I'm in an even worse mood than when I woke up today.

I don't get it. He likes having me in his bed, I like being there, and yet here I am in "my" bed. I don't want this to be my bed or my room or my space. I want to be in his, and I don't fucking understand why I can't be. I think he's just trying to be a dick. It's the only reason

I can think of as to why he denies us both what we want. I did nothing today to warrant punishment. I don't understand him at all.

Other than being irritated, I'm also confused a lot. I've been that way since the first night Nash pulled me away from Troy and took me into the back room at the Underground Club. Nash is a very odd duck. I knew instantly he was. I mean, seriously, what kind of Dom takes a boy back into a fetish room and only asks for a kiss. It's not normal. I tell ya what kind, the type that has a screw loose. Now, don't get me wrong. It was a nice kiss and the guy is smoking hot, but I didn't like how it knocked me off-kilter, and I have to admit, I was pretty disappointed I didn't get so much as a slap or a good fucking.

Nash is a total weirdo.

If Nash thinks he's helping me with my issue with pain, he's not. I could teach him a thing or two about pain. I tried to play the nice, sweet little sub, did all the right things, used all the right words, including safewording, just because I thought it was what Nash wanted to hear. It didn't work. I got so fucking anxious I started thinking about cutting again. I played the role for a while, but each day it gets harder and harder to pretend. He doesn't hit me hard enough or often enough. I don't think he understands what that does to me, how it leaves me feeling empty with too much time to think about things. Things I don't want to think about. Things that should be left in the past. It's getting harder to keep them there. They keep escaping from the iron safe I've constructed. This is my prison. I'm the keeper of the keys, locking bits of me behind cell doors. The safe is where the weapons are held. The lock must hold. The things within will destroy me as surely as a knife would pierce my flesh. No, I'm not going to think of the blade, what it represents, or the release only it can provide me. Goddamn it! If only Nash would get tougher, was a better Dom, then I might not have to wait too long for its kiss. I wouldn't be so angry and confused all the time.

This is his fault.

I feel like an idiot most of the time, and I'm beginning to think Nash is doing that on purpose. But why? Doesn't he know how to take control and be consistent with it? It's easy. He tells me what do to, and I do it or get my ass beat. Plain and simple. Done and done. But he'd rather talk about why I misbehaved. He demands respect. When I want to feel the bite of leather, I disrespect him, but again, he wants to discuss the reasons behind my behavior rather than correct it properly. It's a two-way street—he pushes and I push back. He swings the crop and I take it. Fuck! How can anyone not get it? Maybe it's not me that's fucked-up and stupid, but Nash who has the issues. That's got to be it. Nash is forcing all this shit from my past to come out. He's the one taking me back to a time I don't want to think about. He is the one wielding the lockpick. It will be all his fault when the safe springs open and I reach for the knife. His fault when I finally give in to the need to cut, and oh how that need is growing. To feel that release, to purge myself of all the bad shit, watch it ooze from my body.

When the blood runs from my body, it will be Nash's fault, not mine.

I am not weak.

Nash is simply not strong enough.

Chapter One

A DARK cloud had descended upon Nash's house. It was thick and heavy. No matter how hard he tried, he couldn't seem to push it aside to find what lay beneath it or find the source of it. All he knew was there was something wrong. He couldn't pinpoint exactly what it was, but it was there nonetheless. Over the past week, since he'd taken Joshua to the Underground Club, there had been a definite change in his sub. It had been a good night. They'd spent the evening in the company of others in the lifestyle, watched a great demonstration of fire play, then returned home to a night of blissful shared orgasms. There was no reason he could think of for the change in his boy, but he was definitely different. Joshua completed his chores without question, doing as expected of him, taking his discipline readily, but taking no pleasure in any of it. Nash couldn't decide if Joshua was brooding or distracted. He'd asked him on several occasions: while in the safe room, when he was in a good subspace, early in the morning while snuggling and sleepy, and while hanging out on the couch chitchatting. Each time Joshua would claim there was nothing wrong. He sounded sincere, but there was something. Nash couldn't help but feel as if he was failing. It was his job to know his sub, to know what he needed and take care of said needs. He shouldn't have to ask Joshua what he needed. He should know.

Nash sat up in bed, leaned against the headboard, and ran his fingers through his hair. He blew out a heavy breath of exasperation. There had never been a doubt that things would be difficult with Joshua, considering Joshua's past. Nevertheless, he hadn't expected that every step Joshua took forward, he'd stumble back three. In some aspects, things were going well between them, better than Nash had ever dreamed. In other things, it had gone completely wrong. Until he could figure out why on the latter, he was completely ineffective in fixing the problem.

The bedside clock flashed six. Joshua wouldn't be up and bringing Nash his morning coffee for another thirty minutes. He had time. He grabbed his cell from the bedside table and dialed a familiar number.

Malcolm answered after the first ring. "Good morning, sunshine."

"Hey, Malcolm. Did I catch you at a bad time?"

"No, not at all. Although, the boy I have bent over my knee, waiting for his morning spanking, may disagree."

"Ah, shit. Sorry. I'll call you back later."

"I'm kidding. He's getting my coffee. One cannot redden naughty butts until he's had an adequate amount of caffeine. So, what is so important that you're calling me this early?"

"I was hoping we could meet for lunch today. I'd like to toss a couple things at you," Nash explained.

"Something wrong?"

"I'm not sure. Something is nagging at me, but I can't put my finger on it. Maybe I'm paranoid."

"You sound genuinely worried. I don't detect a hint of the confidence I heard in you the last time we spoke. However, I highly doubt it's paranoia."

"I'm not worried, exactly, not yet anyway. It's more like… I don't know. Maybe I am…. I…. Christ, Malcolm. I'm not even sure about anything anymore. I'm stumped. Let's talk later. My thoughts are a bit foggy. I haven't had my morning cup of joe yet either. Morning spankings aren't the only thing one shouldn't do without an adequate amount of caffeine."

"Agreed. How about noon here at the club?"

"I'll be there and thanks."

Nash ended the call and set his cell back on the table. He tucked his hands behind his head and stared at the ceiling. He felt marginally better. Malcolm had a good read on people. He might not have been around Joshua very much, and Nash didn't have specifics to tell him, but Malcolm was a great sounding board. Even with vague feelings stirring inside Nash, Malcolm might be able to throw out some ideas, stir them up so to speak, and help

Nash move forward toward a path to discovering what was going on with Joshua and what Nash was missing.

While he waited for Joshua to wake and bring his coffee, Nash wandered back through his memories from the first time he met Joshua—picking apart each interaction, every gesture, and nuance of Joshua's demeanor, looking for something, anything to explain the unease he was experiencing. Their first kiss, Nash's anger at Troy and how quickly the Dom had given up Joshua. Each scene, every response Joshua had to both pleasure and pain. Nash even considered each time they simply sat next to each other watching TV or lay on the couch snuggling. There was something there, dammit.

As he analyzed each event, he kept returning to the conversation he'd had with Kirk the first night Nash had taken Joshua into the back room.

"Trust me, that's a hornet's nest you do not want to get tangled up in. That boy is a complete and utter fucking mess."

"What do you mean by mess?"

"He has no limits. Like zero fucking limits."

"That's impossible. Everyone has their limits."

"Not Joshua. He's as bad as a heroin junkie, only his drug of choice is pain. He's constantly looking for the bigger and better high. He'll let you kill him before he'll safeword."

Nash wasn't sure why, but he had a strange feeling his current problem with Joshua could be answered by what Kirk had told him. Over the past couple of months, he'd assumed Kirk was wrong. Nash had been able to easily get Joshua to use his safeword. Joshua wasn't limitless. Nash had found some. Sure, the limits he'd uncovered were small, but still, he'd found them. Hadn't he?

Closing his eyes, Nash concentrated on recalling the moment he'd discovered the first one. He remembered how strong Joshua had been. Nash had never met anyone who could take so many blows without so much as a grunt, an involuntary twitch. How many had he given before he'd gotten a response, six, seven, ten? Nash wasn't sure of the exact number, but he did remember getting a sound. He also recalled the way it had made him feel, his excitement at finding a limit, a small one, but he'd been happy, even cocky. Thinking at the time that Kirk was and idiot. But was he? Or was it Nash who was the idiot?

Seriously, Nash, think about what I said long and hard before you consider playing with that boy. He may not have limits, but I assure you, he will push you to yours.

Nash opened his eyes and reached for his goatee, only then remembering why he'd shaved it off. Each time he was unsure or worried, he'd run it through his thumb and index finger. After Malcolm had pointed it out, Nash had shaved it, worried Joshua would be able to pick up on the tell and use it against him. His chin might be smooth, but he hadn't broken the habit. He dropped his hand onto his lap and played with the sheet instead.

He will push you to yours.

Nash couldn't get the conversation out of his head. The longer he thought about it, the more convinced he was that the current problems could be found within Kirk's warning.

He will push you to yours.

The door creaked, and Nash turned his head to see Joshua coming into the room with a tray, the scent of freshly brewed coffee accompanying him. Maybe with a sufficient amount of caffeine, he could get a grasp on his thoughts.

"Good morning, Joshua."

"Good morning, Sir," Joshua replied. He kept his head bowed, eyes lowered respectfully as he set the tray on Nash's lap, then went to his knees next to the bed.

Nash added cream and sugar to his coffee, then stirred it as he studied Joshua. His posture was perfect, his breathing slow and even, not a single outward physical sign of anything amiss, yet the unease clung to Nash.

He patted the bed next to him. "C'mere, boy."

Joshua rolled to his feet and slid beneath the covers with such grace and ease he barely disturbed the tray.

Sitting shoulder to shoulder, Nash didn't turn toward Joshua, instead took a sip of coffee. It was the perfect temperature, so he took another larger drink. "How did you sleep?"

"Fine."

"I thought I heard you get up a couple of times."

"Yes, Sir."

When Joshua didn't elaborate further, Nash studied him as he finished his coffee. This weird feeling of unease was driving him crazy. He didn't dare ask Joshua what was going on. He doubted he'd get a straight answer. Joshua was always vague these days. Nash also didn't want to give away just how out of sorts he was. His lunch with Malcolm couldn't come soon enough.

"I notice you only brought one mug in. Have you already had your coffee?"

"Yes, Sir."

"What time did you get up?"

"Five."

Nash cocked his head. "I heard you in the bathroom around three, but I didn't hear you get up at five."

"I was quiet, Sir."

"What were you doing?"

"Nothing, Sir."

Okay, this small talk with one-word answers was getting ridiculous. "Is there something you want to talk to me about?" Nash asked.

"No, Sir."

"Then why are you wringing your hands? I can tell there is something bothering you. I wish you would talk to me."

Joshua instantly stilled the movement of his hands. "Nothing to say. I'm fine, Sir, really."

Nash ran his hand up and down Joshua's thigh in a soothing manner. "All right, look. I know you're not being completely honest right now."

Joshua stiffened.

"It's okay, I'm not mad, and I'm not going to force you to tell me what's going on in that pretty head of yours. Not this morning anyway. I will give you a couple days to get it straightened out, but in the meantime, I'm here when you're ready to talk."

Joshua was quiet with a thoughtful expression. Nash added more coffee to his mug from the carafe and added the fixings. Joshua said nothing. The etched lines of tension around Joshua's eyes told Nash that Joshua was thinking about what was weighing heavily on him. Nash wanted nothing more than to demand Joshua tell him, but he held back. He could demand a lot from Joshua. Their contract afforded Nash certain liberties. Forcing Joshua to talk about his past or his innermost feelings wasn't one of the things covered. It was Nash's job to earn his boy's trust so he felt he could share such things. Until then, Nash would have to be patient—not one of his strongest attributes, but he was working on it.

The silence stretched out, not the comfortable kind but the type that was full of tension.

Resigning himself to the fact that Joshua wasn't going to open up and share his thoughts, Nash asked, "What have you prepared for breakfast?" Maybe small talk would lead to something more in depth.

"I made a spinach and swiss quiche. I also cut up some fresh pineapple, kiwi, and strawberries. I hope that's okay, Sir."

"Sounds wonderful. I'm having lunch with Malcolm today, so don't worry about preparing anything."

"Yes, Sir."

Nash sipped his coffee without taking his eyes off Joshua, who steadfastly refused to look at Nash. Once again, the silence became painfully uncomfortable, so goddamn thick Nash nearly choked on it.

"I—"

"It's...."

They looked at each other. Briefly, Nash smiled, but Joshua looked distressed and turned away.

"Sorry, didn't mean to interrupt you, Sir."

"No, it's okay. Go ahead."

"I was thinking. It's just.... The only reason I'm not saying anything is.... Well, I'm trying to work out a few things in my own head. I haven't figured it out yet, so I'm not ready to share until I do, ya know?"

Joshua's words cut Nash like a knife. "Yeah, I do," Nash said, struggling to keep the profound disappointment out of his tone. He did understand it but certainly didn't like it. His boy should be able to share such things, and it was painfully apparent Nash had failed miserably. His poor boy didn't feel as if Nash could help him work through an issue. Nash swallowed down his sigh, kept his face neutral. He tucked a wayward curl behind Joshua's ear, then ran a finger along the soft, dark hair on Joshua's jaw. "I'm here whenever you are ready to talk, okay?"

Joshua pushed into Nash's touch briefly, then seemed to catch himself and pulled away, straightening his posture. "Thank you, Sir."

Again, Nash had to swallow down a sigh. Dammit, not only were they on different pages but oceans apart. If only Joshua would just talk to him. But no matter how much Nash wished otherwise, it wasn't going to happen at the moment. No sense in beating a dead horse. It wouldn't do any damn good and might even push Joshua further away. The one thing he could do was keep Joshua's daily routine normal and hope he came around.

Nash set his mug down, then moved the tray to the nightstand. "All right, boy, get your paddle out of the drawer and let's get this day started."

"Yes, Sir." A spark of excitement lit up Joshua's features. He quickly got up and hurried across the room.

At least Joshua was still happy about something. It was a start. After speaking with Malcolm, hopefully Nash could come up with a clear plan on how to lessen the distance between them.

STANDING AT the stove, heating a can of chicken noodle soup, Joshua clenched his ass and smiled. Maybe he should start keeping his mouth shut more often. It certainly seemed to have put an extra bit of power in Nash's swing during morning discipline. It still wasn't up to the level Joshua liked, but maybe in time, he could manipulate Nash to give him what he wanted. Perhaps then he wouldn't need Dr. Hobson or the stupid journal.

The only thing he wanted was to keep his head down, do his chores, bark when told, and, in turn, get the pain he craved. If he could only obtain that, he wouldn't have to worry about all the other bullshit.

He dipped his spoon and brought it to his lips. "Motherfucker," he yelped and dropped the spoon. It landed in the pot, causing the scalding hot liquid to splash and land on his bare chest. Scrambling, he snatched up a towel and wiped his chest as he cut the stove off. Jesus, how long had he been standing there lost in thought and enjoying the burn in his ass?

"Long enough to create another burn apparently." He chuckled, then winced as his tongue throbbed.

Joshua grabbed a bowl from the cupboard, scooped out some soup, and took it to the table. He was actually in a pretty good mood, something he should be experiencing a lot more of than he had been of late. Oh, he'd settled in at Nash's home, one of the finest places he'd ever lived. Nash was nicer than most people Joshua had ever dealt with. He should love it. The good vibes should be a daily thing. Hell, he should be feeling that way twenty-four seven. If he was normal, he would be, but Lord knew he was beyond the range of normal. Like the sting in his ass, his good mood was temporary. It was the crash after the high that was the real bitch.

He wasn't even sure if the high was worth it anymore.

Chapter Two

LEANING BACK in the butter-soft leather chair, Nash brought the brandy glass to his nose and sniffed the deep fruity and woody aroma. He took a sip, the flavor smooth like a liquid flame. It was no shock that the ever fashionable and refined Malcolm had introduced Nash to the delight. What was surprising was that after an hour and a wonderful meal of baked salmon and rice pilaf with Malcolm, Nash was no closer to figuring out what the hell was going on with Joshua.

Malcolm settled farther into his chair and studied Nash. "I do not doubt your instincts. I only wonder if you're looking at this situation with Joshua objectively."

"What is that supposed to mean?"

"Only that I know you care deeply for the boy, and given his difficult past…."

Malcolm swirled his brandy around in his glass, staring at the movement of the dark liquid. He'd left his words hanging in the air, and Nash knew Malcolm well enough to know that he was searching for the right words and it would do absolutely no good to interrupt him or push him. He'd speak when he was ready and only when he was ready. Nash took the opportunity to enjoy his brandy, although his anxiety over Joshua and wanting to get to the heart of the problem did make it a challenge. Of course he cared deeply for Joshua. Nash had never been drawn to anyone like he was Joshua. He also had never felt as protective or possessive over anyone. Nash would do anything for his boy, and it was frustrating as hell not being able to figure out what he could do to help.

After what felt like an eternity, Malcolm finally finished his sentence. "Do you think that perhaps you're seeing and feeling things simply because you feel sorry for him?"

Nash considered Malcolm's words for a moment. Sure, he felt bad for the way Joshua's life had started out and continued to spiral down as he grew. He'd been bounced around from one home to another, never knowing peace and security as a child. As a young adult, it only became worse. One man after another betrayed him, used him. But was Joshua's hard life the reason behind Nash's unease? Was he really making something out of nothing?

When Nash didn't respond, Malcolm added, "Let me ask you this. Are you afraid of giving Joshua what he needs because you fear becoming one of the abusers?"

The outrage that rushed through Nash caused him to sit up so quickly he nearly spilled his drink. "How dare you? I would never abuse him," he said defensively.

Malcolm glared at him. "I suggest you adjust your tone. I am not the enemy here. I merely asked if you were worried about it."

It took a couple clicks of the clock for the anger to seep from Nash, but finally, he slumped back in his chair. "I'm sorry. I know you're trying to help. I'm so goddamn frustrated that I can't figure this out. Still, it was unfair of me to lash out at you. It's more proof of how out of sorts I am."

"I know you would never abuse him, but sometimes our subconscious thoughts can derail even the best of intentions," Malcolm pointed out. "Perhaps you're soft on him, worrying about things that aren't an issue because you feel sorry for him."

This wasn't the first time Malcolm had asked him this. Nash's reaction was the same as it had been the last time, outrage. That, in and of itself, was telling. The fact that such a question could anger him so quickly meant there was something behind it. At least it was worth considering. Taking a deep breath, Nash worked to let go of the anger and find some calm. It took several more deep breaths and finishing his brandy before he achieved it. Only then did he dare speak.

"I can see why you would think I feel sorry for him. Poor guy was dealt a shit hand from day one. But honestly, Malcolm, I don't think that is what has me all in knots today. However, I will concede that I may be too soft on him."

"And if it isn't you feeling sorry for him that is driving this reaction, do you have any ideas as to what may be causing it?"

The tension Nash had created between them cleared, and once again they were two equals searching for a common solution.

"Curiosity? My consuming need to know everything. My lack of a clear-cut plan. Take your pick."

Malcolm thrummed his fingers against the arm of his chair. "Let's start with the first one. Curiosity?"

"Each time Joshua sees Cedric, I ask him how it went and he says fine, then shuts himself in his room. It's driving me crazy not knowing. Even worse, I hate that he doesn't trust me enough to share it with me." Nash pointed a finger at Malcolm. "And before you say it, yes, I know I have to earn his trust, and I'm trying. It's just frustrating that it seems to be taking so damn long."

"And patience has never been your strongest attribute," Malcolm said slyly.

"No, but I have kick-ass organizational skills," Nash grumbled.

"I'll give you that. Okay, on to the next concern. Your obsessive need to know everything."

Nash set his empty glass down on the coffee table, then sat back and crossed his legs. "I don't really see that as a problem. I'd say it's a good attribute to have in both my professional and personal life. The difficulty lies when I don't know."

"And when it comes to Joshua, that, like the trust, will come in time."

Nash clamped down on the urge to roll his eyes. Malcolm made it sound sensible and easy. It was neither. Malcolm was correct on one thing so far—Nash's patience was not the best. It was definitely something he needed to work on. Having some would be no doubt invaluable in dealing with Joshua. However, it wasn't like he could run down to the corner store and pick up a bottle of instant patience.

"You should try yoga and meditation. It might help you with that grumpy disposition you've been sporting lately."

This time Nash did roll his eyes, but he hid the evidence by tilting his head back and looking up at the ceiling. "Ha-ha."

"I'm serious," Malcolm insisted. "It may help you find some balance within yourself."

Nash dropped his head and gave Malcolm a skeptical look. "And you know this how?"

"It's all the rage. The boys talk about it all the time. They say it helps them with their focus and find calm in between sessions."

"If they had a good Dom, they wouldn't need all that mumbo jumbo," Nash countered.

Malcolm didn't laugh. Instead, he looked at Nash with a serious expression. "And sometimes it's a tool that could help a sub and a Dom who are struggling." He waved a dismissive hand. "Anyway, think about it."

Nash's first inclination was to dismiss the idea. However, if it could help, he'd try to keep an open mind. "I'll think about it."

Malcolm nodded toward Nash's empty glass. "Would you like more?"

"No thanks. It was good, but I better keep my head."

"Good idea. So we come to the last item on your list. Your lack of a plan."

"And right back to the main reason for my visit." Nash sighed. "How can I come up with a plan if I don't know what the hell is wrong? I just want him to talk to me."

"Hey, I may have a solution. Didn't you say Joshua had no friends or family?"

"Yeah."

"Then maybe the problem lies in his social skills."

Nash cocked his head. "I'm not following you."

"Joshua has spent his adult years being told what to do, and he does so in order to get something in return. He's basically going to do what you tell him, and for that gets a reward. He's not going to discuss something that may upset you or that he's not sure how it will play out. He's jeopardizing the reward."

"Okay, so how do I make him realize talking will be rewarding?"

"You can't. At least not by simply telling him."

Nash laid his head back and blew out a heavy breath. "Great. Back to square one." He jerked upright when a heavy hand landed on his thigh. "What the hell, Malcolm?"

"Now that I have your attention, would you mind if I finish speaking without interruption?" Malcolm arched a single brow.

Nash rubbed his leg, kept his mouth shut, and nodded.

"As I was saying, you can't make him see the reward in opening up to you, not when he's so conflicted. What he needs is someone who is an equal and has experienced many of the same things or at least has had difficulties with the whole reward system. He needs a confidant. A friend."

"I'm his friend," Nash insisted.

"No, you're his Dom, provider, and lover who wants to be his friend." Malcolm shook his head. "But you're not. Perhaps one day you will be, but again, that will come in time."

Nash doubted he could find a friend for Joshua on the shelf sitting next to Nash's can of patience at the corner store. He also couldn't say, *Hey, Joshua, go get yourself a friend to bring home*. Friendship took time to develop and was based on a connection. "Okay, so where do you suggest I look for this friend and confidant?"

Malcolm pushed to his feet with a large satisfied grin on his face. "I just so happen to have one you can borrow."

"I'm serious, Malcolm."

"As am I. Now get up, and we'll go talk to the boy and see if he's interested."

"Joshua has an appointment with Cedric this afternoon." Nash checked his watch but went to his feet as instructed. "We'll have to wait till later."

Malcolm slung his arm around Nash and patted his back. "Not Joshua, the friend."

Nash allowed Malcolm to lead him out of the room. Malcolm did things on his own terms and at his own pace. So Nash simply followed. He'd find out soon enough what this big plan was. He only hoped it was one of Malcolm's better ones. Nash's nerves depended on it.

"You seem especially quiet today," Dr. Hobson pointed out.

Joshua continued to stare at his hands, picking at a hangnail on the side of his thumb. "I'm just tired."

"Physically or mentally?"

"Does it really matter?" Joshua asked. He wasn't in the mood to talk or be analyzed like a goddamn science project. If he'd any sense, he would have feigned illness or some such excuse to skip his appointment today. But it was too late. He was already under the microscope and Dr. Hobson's scrutinizing gaze.

"Of course it matters. If you were simply up late and didn't get any sleep, that is one thing. However, if you were unable to sleep because of something weighing heavily on you, then we need to address it."

Joshua crossed his arms over his chest stubbornly. "I don't want to be here."

"Then why did you come?"

Joshua lifted his head and glared at the shrink. "Because I didn't have any choice."

"Sure you do," Dr. Hobson said calmly, not reacting to Joshua's angry demeanor. "You are a grown man. You have a choice in what you do."

"I'm a fucking sub. I don't get a choice. I do what I'm told, period."

"Is Nash forcing you to be his sub?" Dr. Hobson inquired calmly.

Joshua gawked at him in utter surprise. "Of course not!" What a ridiculous question. He'd been elated when Troy had given him to Nash. The only thing he missed was Troy's heavy hand and sadistic ways. However, having to live with him and his preferred boy in such a small space had been beyond trying.

"I'm sure you're aware then, in choosing to be Nash's submissive, you hold power. Same as you hold power as to whether you want to be here or not."

"I have the power? Yeah, right." Joshua laughed bitterly. He sure didn't feel like he was in control, and he certainly felt powerless.

If he had any, he'd be able to stop the old memories from creeping in. They showed up whenever they wanted.

"Joshua," Dr. Hobson said gently. "Look at me."

Joshua hadn't even realized he was once again staring at his hands. Only this time, they were curled into tight fists. He tentatively lifted his gaze and met Dr. Hobson's.

"No one, and I do mean no one, can make you do anything you don't allow. Each time Nash binds you, it's because you allowed him. Each time he takes a crop or flogger to you, he does so because you allowed him. You service him, care for him, and give him your submission by choice."

Joshua started to protest but snapped his mouth shut before he could. Dr. Hobson was right. Joshua had *chosen* to sign the contract with Nash. He had *agreed* to sever his ties with Troy as long as another Dom took him on. He had his safeword. He could stop any scene at any time he wanted.

Then why do I feel so goddamn powerless?

Was it merely the past producing those feelings, or was there more to it? The moments stretched out as he considered the questions, but the only thing he got for his efforts was a throb in his temples.

Joshua leaned his head back against the soft leather chair and stared up at the ceiling. "I feel even more fucked-up than I did when I walked in here. You're not doing a very good job, Doc," Joshua said, trying to tease, but he failed miserably. He sounded sad even to his own ears.

"I'm simply trying to make you think about your choices and—"

"That's the problem right there."

"Meaning?" Dr. Hobson asked.

"I don't want to think. Thinking is dangerous. I just want someone to set up my day, tell me what to do, and do all the thinking for me."

"You're not a robot, Joshua."

No, he wasn't. Joshua understood he was made of flesh and bone and given free will. Only he wished it were programs and software that controlled his day. Maybe then he could pray for his circuit board to fry or his battery to run out.

~*~

Today was another frustrating day with dear old Doctor Headshrink. He didn't ask me about what I wrote since the last time I saw him. I'm shocked. I'm even more surprised that I'm actually sitting here writing to myself again. I still think it's really fucking stupid. Then again, I'm really fucking stupid, so why not write in this journal? Doc brought up something today that I'm having a hard time swallowing….

I'm in power.

Even thinking it or writing it makes me want to laugh. Only, it's not the least bit funny. I do have a choice. I am the one who gives Nash the permission to do to me what he wants. Yet I've never felt more powerless than I do right now. It makes me question my conviction that all the old ugly memories I've been dealing with are Nash's fault. How can it be if I'm in power? Fuck, I hate that word.

Why doesn't anything make sense anymore?

Why am I even here?

Chapter Three

WHEN JOSHUA walked out of Cedric's office, Nash instantly knew it hadn't gone well. Joshua's shoulders were slumped, head down, and he stiffly slid into the passenger seat of the car. Of course, when Nash asked him how he was, Joshua had answered, "Fine." Nash was beginning to really hate that word. *Fine* described china, silks, and dining, not sessions with a psychiatrist.

The minute they'd arrived home, Joshua bolted for his room, and the sound of the lock being engaged was like a dagger to Nash's heart. Now, with Joshua still hidden from him, Nash sat on pins and needles, waiting for his boy to emerge.

The heavy cloud that had descended upon his home a week ago thickened further with each passing day, each passing hour. It was so thick Nash was practically choking on it. He couldn't take a deep breath, couldn't seem to relax the tension in his muscles, nor could he release the vise that was squeezing his chest. It was driving him nuts.

Nash pushed up off the couch and started to pace. That tension in his body made his movements awkward and jerky, so much so that he misjudged his step and tripped over the side table next to the recliner. Pain radiated from his left big toe all the way up to his gut.

"Son of a bitch!" he growled under his breath and limped into the kitchen.

He snatched open the fridge. His first thought was to grab the bottle of Wild Turkey he'd stashed in the freezer. The next second he thought better of it. He needed to keep his head. Joshua was going to need Nash to be sober when he finally opened the door. If he opened the door today. *Ugh!* He took a bag of frozen peas for a pain reliever instead and hobbled back to the couch. He propped his feet up on the coffee table and placed the veggies on his throbbing toe.

Dammit!

Now he was confused, grumpy, *and* in pain. He hated being so screwed up. Somehow, he had to come up with something. He and Joshua couldn't keep going like this. The problem was, Nash had no idea how to help either of them. The helpless feeling was the worst to deal with.

Since he'd first started dabbling in the lifestyle, he'd been confident in who and what he was. Even while submitting to Malcolm all those years ago, Nash had known he was dominant. He'd had a clear-cut plan, a vision as to where his life was headed and how he was going to live it. And with that plan, he'd found much success, both personally and professionally as a financial advisor. He'd done so by being able to get inside the heads of other people, especially submissives. To know what they were feeling and what they needed. Joshua changed all that.

For the first time in his life, Nash had no idea where he was headed, and the uncertainty was shaking him to his very core. It was ironic that the one man Nash wanted to be the best for, the one man he was falling in love with, was also the one man Nash couldn't read or know how to help.

Nash laid his head back and closed his eyes. Surprisingly, rather than Joshua's face in his mind's eye, it was Kirk's face, and his voice whispered, *"He may not have any limits, but he'll push you to yours."*

Nash's eyes flew open, and he jerked upright as the realization hit him like a ton of bricks.

The perfect posture.

The ease with which safewords slipped from a tongue.

Brooding.

Anger.

Tears.

Joshua was manipulating him. Nash knew it as sure as he was sitting here. He'd allowed his pride to cloud his better judgment. He'd thought himself better than everyone else who had dealt with Joshua. He wasn't. Joshua was a pain slut, had been for years. Nash wasn't dealing with that fact, but ignoring it. How many days had Nash denied Joshua what he craved?

Only now was it dawning on Nash that the days he'd denied Joshua were the most difficult days to read, to understand his boy. It had been after a period of time without punishment that Joshua had confided in Nash about the self-mutilation. To further Nash's outrage at himself, Malcolm's question popped into Nash's head. *"Are you sure you don't feel sorry for him?"*

Nash leaned forward and buried his head in his hands. This was his fault. He did feel sorry for Joshua. He was allowing his boy's past to guide his hand rather than being what Joshua needed in the here and now. He was ignoring the glaring signs of manipulation. Joshua had used Nash's love, pity, and pride against him.

"How could I have been so foolish?" he muttered.

After long moments of wallowing in self-pity and mentally kicking himself in the ass, Nash lifted his head, a new resolve settling within him. He refused to let Joshua manipulate him a minute longer. In allowing such behavior, he was letting Joshua down. It wasn't only Cedric's job to help Joshua once a week, but Nash's job to do it every single day.

Nash pushed to his feet and headed to his office. He needed pen and paper, needed lists, a plan. The first thing was to take Malcolm's advice and set up a lunch date between Joshua and Denny. Joshua needed a peer, someone he could confide in until Nash earned the right to be Joshua's confidant. Nash wasn't sure about his next step, other than he had to be consistent and strict with Joshua, yet loving and thoughtful in his daily routine with his boy. And Joshua was his boy. Nash only had to work harder to deserve that privilege.

JOSHUA WAS surprised at how draining writing his thoughts could be. He was tired in his head, in his heart, in his very soul. He slid the notebook between the mattress and box spring, then stretched out on the bed and buried himself in his pillow and blankets. The questions and doubt assaulted him until he wanted to scream.

He knew Nash was waiting, would be getting hungry. Joshua should be pulling his sorry ass up out of bed and preparing dinner, but he couldn't. Not yet. He could only lie there, paralyzed by the self-loathing, as the questions he'd been trying to answer became accusations.

The whole concept of being the one in the position of power wasn't sitting well with him. Logically, he understood how the whole Dominant/submissive relationship worked. He was a submissive but also a grown man and, as such, consented to the whims of his Dominant.

Whims? Is that the appropriate term to use?

Joshua considered it briefly and then just as quickly let it go. It didn't matter what term he used for what Dominants did or how they behaved. The important thing was that he accepted being on the receiving end of it. Again, the notion of being in control caused him to cringe. He shifted and buried himself farther beneath his covers. If only he could hide from himself and the world as easily. Hell, at the moment, he'd settle for being able to turn his brain off for a while. But of course he didn't know where the off switch was located, so the conversation with Dr. Hobson replayed in his head until he wondered at what point in his life said power became his.

It certainly wasn't when his mother chose to stick a needle in her arm rather than take care of him. Nor was it when he was passed around from one foster home to another. He'd have loved to have been adopted into a true home of his own. That never happened; instead, he wound up on the streets, selling his ass for a meal and a bed. That wasn't power either, but desperation. Even during his first experience in the lifestyle, he hadn't been the one with the power. Sure, he had chosen to walk in the club, climb onto the stage, and allow someone to hit him. However, it had been his love of the adrenaline rush that had propelled him up those stairs. The rush had been in control, not him. Christ, he was no better than his mother. He just had a different drug of choice. Even now, he had to wonder if his need for pain was the true driving force behind his actions. Had he truly ever had any power?

Nash, on the other hand, definitely seemed in control of his life and his surroundings. He had all the things Joshua had hoped for when he was young—a nice house, a good job, friends, and respect. Maybe it wasn't such a bad thing to allow someone like Nash to be the boss. Joshua considered it. The longer he thought about it, the more conflicted he became. Twenty-five years of failure wasn't a great track record, but if he gave all the power to Nash, then he'd have to deal with unwanted memories. He could do worse than having Nash as his Dom and calling all the shots, a lot worse. And still he hesitated. Reliving nightmares of what happened when a Dom had all the power could destroy him. It nearly had.

Chapter Four

LEANING AGAINST the doorjamb to the dining room, Nash watched Joshua carefully as he moved in and out of the kitchen while preparing dinner. He looked thoughtful, but Nash didn't see any signs of true distress. He'd asked his boy how he was when he'd first come out of his room, only to once again get *"Fine."* Nash's frustration had gotten the better of him, and he'd snapped. The word was no longer allowed to pass Joshua's lips. In fact, Joshua wasn't allowed to speak unless Nash asked him a direct question. Nash was done being soft on his boy. They would work this out one way or another. They were going to get back on a schedule, and new rules would be set, ones that Joshua would follow or face correction. Nash was done walking on eggshells and second-guessing himself. It wasn't what either of them needed. They needed strict and clear-cut rules, discipline, and consistency. Without those things, neither of them would ever be truly settled or happy.

Joshua appeared with two glasses of ice water, silverware, and napkins, which he set on the table. Nash took note of Joshua's breathing. It was deep and even. There were no outward indicators of distress or unease. Nash knew not to rely too heavily on this. Joshua was a complicated person and being such, there was no telling what was going on in his mind. It changed from moment to moment. Hell, from second to second. Nash had to be content in his own determination and plans going forward.

"Dinner is ready, Sir," Joshua said before he disappeared into the kitchen.

Nash pushed off the wall and made it to the table before Joshua reemerged with a plate of baked cheese ravioli in a spicy-smelling red sauce that he set in front of Nash, along with a crusty garlic bread. He slipped back into the kitchen and returned with a plate for himself, which he set down at his place. He sat opposite Nash, laid a napkin on his lap, then sat up straight, eyes respectfully lowered and waited.

Nash picked up his fork and used it to cut the tender stuffed pasta. A delicious scent wafted upward, and Nash's stomach growled in response. He brought his fork to his mouth, took a bite, and practically moaned at the wonderful flavor. It tasted even better than it smelled. "This is very good, boy."

Joshua smiled broadly and picked up his fork. "Thank you." Joshua jerked his head up, eyes going wide and snapped his mouth shut. He just as quickly lowered his gaze then sighed. "That wasn't a question. I'm sorry, Sir."

"It will take some getting used to. Two strokes. The first for announcing dinner." Nash kept his voice calm and matter-of-fact. He took another bite of pasta, leisurely enjoying his meal before continuing. "After dinner you are to clear the table and do the dishes. Once the kitchen is clean, my bedding is to be changed and the bedroom dusted. In the morning, you will wake me as usual and then make breakfast. You will have your morning discipline, then perform your routine chores. Through all of this, you will speak only when I say you may. Questions?" He picked up his water glass and waited, eyes on Joshua.

Joshua paused, a thoughtful expression on his face. "Yes, Sir. I'm not sure how well I'm going to do. I mean, after I clean your room, what then? I normally ask you what you want me to do next. I won't know whether I return to my room or stay near you? What if I think you may need something? Should I just ignore it, not worry about it? How am I supposed to take care of your needs if I can't ask what they are?" Joshua huffed out a heavy breath. "I'm not very good at guessing. I need direction."

Nash sipped his water for a moment as he considered each of Joshua's concerns and questions then nodded. "I know this is going to be difficult for you, but I'm also confident you can do it. That being said, don't anticipate me, simply watch, wait, and respond when I speak. Other than your regular chores, you don't have to think about anything. You only have to be. You are to kneel next to me unless I give you other instructions. If you need to use the bathroom, go. If you are cold, uncomfortable, or in distress, by all means, speak. If you are unsure of anything, ask. What you can't do is question my orders. If you can't do something for any reason, you are to say *yellow* and we'll discuss it." Nash ate some more ravioli before going on. "I want to start my day with you kneeling next to my bed with coffee waiting. I like seeing your face and a steaming mug when I open my eyes. Any other questions?"

Joshua barely hid his smile and answered simply, "No, Sir."

"Wonderful. Now, I'm going to finish this." He pointed his fork toward the pasta, smiled, and stabbed another ravioli. "Because seriously, this is really good, boy."

Joshua said nothing in response this time but silently finished his meal. Knowing they wouldn't be going to the playroom later, he ate well. Usually, he ate lightly when he thought they were going to play. Joshua's excitement had a way of suppressing his appetite. He took another sip of his water and then stood. He moved slowly to Nash's side and knelt beside the chair. With one hand Nash gently stroked Joshua's hair; other than that, he ignored Joshua until he'd finished his meal.

He swallowed the last of his water, wiped is mouth on his napkin then dropped it on his empty plate before going to his feet. "Thank you, boy. I will see you in my office once you've finished cleaning up." Without looking back, Nash left the dining room. Once seated at his desk, he opened the files he was planning to review and stared at them, a slow smile crossing his face. It felt good. Right. He was half-hard from just doing what he needed, and he actually felt himself let go of a lot of his fears about pushing Joshua too hard. Nash set about doing his paperwork, but it was difficult to concentrate on work. Instead, he focused on the distant clattering of dishes and running water as Joshua moved around the kitchen. Before long the house went quiet again. Joshua appeared in the office a few minutes later with freshly brewed coffee. He set the streaming mug down on Nash's desk then wordlessly went to his knees next to Nash's chair.

Nash acknowledged Joshua with a soft touch to his hair. With Joshua near, Nash was able to turn is attention to his work. With the paperwork finished, he sat back in his chair and sipped the coffee.

"Thank you, boy," he said, once more stroking Joshua's hair. "Please go get showered. When you're done, we'll deal with your punishment and talk for a little while."

Joshua started to rise, then hesitated. "I'm sorry, Sir. I have a question."

"Ask," Nash ordered, curious.

"I… well, I don't want to ruin the ring in the shower, Sir. Would you prefer me to remove it?"

Nash grinned. "Good boy. Thank you for thinking about my property." He motioned for Joshua to stand. Nash removed the ring, taking a few moments to play with Joshua's cock. "Very nice. I'm aware that it's even nicer when it's warm, hard, and lathered up." He stroked Joshua again and cupped the heavy balls. "It's also mine and as such you are allowed to wash it but that is it. In fact, you're not to jerk off unless I give you permission to do so."

"Y… yes, Sir," Joshua answered with a stutter, sounding a bit unsure of his answer. Yet, Nash had no doubt Joshua would follow Nash's order.

"Good. Except it wasn't a question, so that's another stroke. Now go shower."

Color flared in Joshua's cheeks and annoyed expression on his face. "Wait, I have another question," Joshua snapped. He caught himself quickly, lowered his eyes, and adjusted his tone to one that was more respectful before he continued. "I'm sorry, Sir. I'm confused and need clarification."

Nash didn't call Joshua for snapping, giving him credit for reining it in quickly. "Ask."

"It feels weird not recognize your orders verbally. Don't you want me to acknowledge them at all?" He sounded frustrated.

Nash leaned back in his chair and considered it for a moment. "When I give an order, it is enough that you merely do it. Accepting my will is a huge part of what I need from you. You are only to speak when I ask you a direct question or want verbal acknowledgment. I trust you'll let me know if you're uncomfortable with an order and I don't mean that kind of discomfort that comes from being pushed or stepping outside your comfort zone, but the type you feel could damage you mentally, emotionally, or physically, you are free to refuse." He smiled softly. "You may not be feeling confident right now, but I am. I know you can do this and be what I need. Questions?"

Joshua seemed to relax with Nash's explanation. "No, Sir," Joshua answered, sounding a bit more sure. His boy really did need a lot of direction.

"Okay. Go take your shower."

Joshua left, his steps sounding lightly as he moved down the hall. Nash smiled as he fingered the cock ring and went to his room to fetch the crop. There was a bite to the anticipation, a joy that had been lacking until now. He turned the crop over and over, felt the weight against his palm, and smiled again. He'd lost the thrill of this somewhere along the way, but it was back. Thank God and he was going to enjoy the fuck out of his time with Joshua tonight.

When Joshua finally reappeared from his shower, he looked more relaxed and smelled of soap and shaving cream. He stopped in the doorway, and his gaze lingered on the crop.

"Hands against the wall, ass out," Nash ordered.

Joshua settled into position, a flush of color blooming out over his skin.

"Three strokes," Nash moved to stand behind Joshua and took a moment to admire his boy, appreciating the lines of his body and the curve of his ass, so nicely offered up. He felt a tightening in his groin. "Three strokes." He took a deep breath. "Ready?"

Joshua nodded. "Yes, Sir."

Nash struck. The first blow landed hard, the line it raised immediate. Joshua gasped with the sting of it and seemed to hold his breath. Nash hesitated. His gaze settled on the network of white scars that stood out in stark contrast to the blooming red line. *So much abuse. Such unnecessary pain.* Nash's gut roiled, bile threatened, but he swallowed it down. He wasn't doing this out of some sick need to hurt, terrorize, and damage. He closed his eyes for a fraction of a moment. *This is about us. What* we *need. What* we *want.* Nash opened his eyes and in quick succession, he laid a second, then third stroke, just above the first. Joshua let his air out in a rush.

"Good boy," Nash praised.

Joshua remained dutifully silent.

Nash studied the red welts carefully. Satisfied he hadn't broken skin, he stepped back and set the crop down on the dresser. He retrieved the cock ring, his own shaft surprisingly extremely hard. If he didn't get himself under control, Joshua wouldn't be the only one needing a ring. Nash smiled. The night was going pleasingly well, and it felt amazing to be moving them forward in a positive and oh so sexy manner. "Turn and display, boy," he said, sitting on the edge of the bed as Joshua turned to face him. Joshua put his arms behind his back and his shoulders squared nicely.

"How do you feel?" Nash asked. He ran his finger gently down the length of Joshua's hard cock.

"Good, Sir," Joshua said. "Focused, calm."

"Good. Tomorrow will be hard. I want you to know that I understand that. Also, this isn't something I'm doing lightly. We both have needs, and I have a duty to make sure they are fulfilled. I promised I would help you find your limits and work through them. I can't promise to make it a pleasant journey, however. I want you to spend some time tonight preparing yourself for it. Do you have any questions at the moment?"

Joshua only asked one question. "Do you need anything before you turn in, Sir?"

"No. Thank you for asking." Nash stood up and secured Joshua's cock into the ring. "You'll be sleeping in your room."

"Yes, Sir." Joshua's shoulders slumped, and there was disappointment in his tone.

"You did well today, boy," Nash said softly. Then he tipped Joshua's head up by his chin and kissed him gently, sucking on his lower lip for a brief moment before pulling away. "Keep it up, and you'll earn a place in my bed in no time."

Joshua opened his mouth, presumably to respond to the praise, but bit down on his lip instead and walked to the door.

Nash had to clamp down on the urge to call Joshua back after seeing his boy's reaction to being sent to his room. He had to stay strong, not only for himself but for Joshua as well. He undressed and got ready for bed. He made sure the alarm was set, though he hoped he wouldn't need it, and then he turned out the lights in the hall and in the room. He disliked the empty spot next to him in bed, and he had to remind himself that there was a damn good reason for it. With a sigh, he rolled over and waited for sleep to overtake him.

Chapter Five

HAVING CHECKED and double-checked that the bindings around Joshua's ankles and wrists weren't too tight, Nash stepped back and admired his handiwork. His boy was tied to the spanking bench, facedown with his hands and feet resting on the floor, his firm ass at the perfect height for caressing, striking, and fucking. Nash had taken extra time in tying Joshua to the bench, not only to be sure he didn't cause Joshua any unnecessary pain, but also to give Nash time to get in the right frame of mind. He had to work to block out the ugly scars that covered Joshua's torso and legs and see only the man beneath the roadmap of torture. It wasn't as hard as Nash had thought. Not to say it was easy, but Joshua was much more than his past.

So much more.

Nash was ashamed that he'd forgotten that, but no more. He ran the tip of his index finger down from the base of Joshua's neck to the crack of his ass. Nash smiled wryly when his touch caused Joshua to shudder and goose bumps to bloom across his flesh.

"Cold?"

"No, Sir. It tickles."

"Enjoy it now. I won't be so gentle in a moment."

"Whatever pleases you, Sir." Joshua tensed, obviously remembering he wasn't supposed to respond.

Once again, Nash cut Joshua some slack for his infraction, given he'd recovered quickly and realized his mistake. Nash had other things to concentrate on, like the flat tone of Joshua's voice. He was saying it for Nash's benefit, not his own or because he believed it. How could Nash not have noticed it before? What other clues to Joshua's manipulative ways had he missed?

No matter. He noticed this one and planned not only to find all the clues but to solve the entire mystery. With purpose, Nash measured his steps, deliberate as he walked across the silent room to the cabinet. He opened it and studied the contents. It was for show. Nash already knew he was going to use the short bamboo cane, but was doing this for Joshua's benefit. Give him time to wonder, let the anticipation grow. Nash tested several implements on his leather-covered thigh. He kept Joshua in his peripheral sight, the even rise and fall of his back quickening ever so slightly the only indication that Joshua's excitement was growing. He returned the flogger he'd been testing, took a lube pack and condom from the shelf, then grabbed the cane before closing the cabinet doors.

He moved close to Joshua again. "Your mind is mine." He ran the tip of the cane down Joshua's back. "Your body is mine. Mine to strike, because it pleases me." He skimmed the cane along Joshua's taut ass and the muscles reacted, flexed. "Mine to stroke and to fuck, because it pleases me," Nash whispered.

Joshua took in a breath sharply as the cane tickled against the sensitive skin of his ass, but made no other sound. He kept his body still, freely giving himself over to Nash's will.

Nash nodded. Confident that Joshua was comfortable and finding a calm headspace, Nash moved around Joshua without speaking. He randomly touched the inside thigh of one leg, his back, his arms with the cane.

"There is only me, Joshua. No anger, no confusion, nothing beyond this room that can touch you. Think about what you want to be, what you can be when you give yourself to me."

Joshua's back gently rose and fell with each breath. Head turned to the side, Joshua rested his cheek on the leather bench, his lips parted as he breathed evenly. He was the picture of relaxation, but the flush of color along his skin as well as the occasional involuntary twitch of a muscle betrayed the illusion. Still, he was beautiful. Nash moved to stand near Joshua's bound legs and gently brushed the cane against the backs of Joshua's thighs and ass. Slowly but steadily, he swung the cane, not really putting any strength behind it, tapping, warming his skin. A low sound rumbled up from deep in Joshua's chest as the contact of the cane increased.

It was a content, peaceful sound. Nash continued a slow buildup, restraining his strength, keeping his strokes light but quick. He moved in a cyclical pattern, down Joshua's left leg, across his ass, up his right leg, and then followed the same pattern in reverse. Before long, the constant repetition painted a wonderful pink color across Joshua's flesh. As the color rose, so did Joshua's pleasurable sounds. The melody grew louder, becoming guttural as it peaked, and then complete stillness and silence. Joshua was flying. Nash continued his pattern, slowly lessening his strokes until they were whispers of touches before stopping altogether.

JOSHUA'S SKIN tingled; there was no longer any real pain as the cane made its rounds, just warmth, heating his skin. As the strokes continued, Joshua's focus narrowed. He could feel the bamboo as it caressed his skin briefly before sliding away. Then nothing. It was as if he had entered a state of suspended animation. Time, place, even his physical body ceased to exist, and he floated. There was no sound, not the whisper of his breath nor the beat of his heart, just complete and utter silence. There were no smells, no sights, nothing but a swirling of strangely muted colors dancing around him.

How long Joshua floated, he didn't know, nor did he care. For the first time in his life, he understood what true peace was. Not just peace like what could be achieved with a quiet, warm bath or a deep dreamless sleep, but a peace Joshua felt in the pit of his soul. He floated and just was.

A carefully measured sound was the first thing he became aware of, and he tried to ignore it. A strange pressure pushed at the cloud of color that surrounded him, increasing as it attempted to invade at random intervals. Joshua winced, momentarily frightened when a loud roar filled his ears, until he realized it was the sound of his own beating heart and the air moving in and out of his lungs. A tingling. A heaviness to the cloud, and then the slap. Joshua gasped when, in a blink, he fell back into his body, and he was aware of someone stroking the skin of his thighs, the sensation almost too much to bear, as if all his nerve endings had come alive at once. Panic began to surge through Joshua's system, and then he heard Nash's low, familiar voice.

"I'm here. Come back to me, Joshua." His voice was calm and soothing. The whispered touch of Nash's fingers was replaced by a stronger, deeper touch along the insides of his thighs, sending sparks dancing along his skin.

Joshua took in a deep breath, blowing it out as the tingling sensation increased. He swallowed, licking his dry lips.

"That's it," Nash purred. "Come back to me."

Nash's warm breath tickled the side of Joshua's neck as he whispered in his ear. "Open your eyes, Joshua."

Even the filtered light through his closed lids seemed harsh, and he squeezed his eyes tightly against the unwanted stimulus.

"Open your eyes, Joshua," Nash urged quietly against his ear.

Slowly, Joshua blinked open his eyes, and it was as if the last switch on an electrical panel had been flipped and all of Joshua's systems were back online, firing at once. The air rushed out of his lungs in a whoosh, and he gasped at the intensity of the sensations racing through him.

"Oh God," he moaned, the sound raw and gravelly from his dry throat.

Nash's warm lips against his ear set off a chain reaction. The tingling raced down his body, and Joshua became keenly aware of the straps tightly wound around his ankles and wrists, the even tighter band surrounding his painfully throbbing cock, and the heaviness in his balls as they drew up snug against his body.

"Tell me what you need," Nash encouraged.

"Oh God... Sir?" he panted, not even sure what he was saying. He was so fucking turned on, it felt as if he would burst.

Nash nuzzled his neck. "Tell me."

"You... fuck.... Sir! Take me." He was babbling; he knew he was but couldn't help it. He needed to come, now!

The growl that erupted from Nash was a deep, animal sound, mingling with Joshua's desperate, needy moans and whimpers and filling the room. "Christ," Nash groaned, moving quickly to position himself behind Joshua's spread and bound legs.

"Please, please…." Joshua panted harshly and then cried out when a slick finger stabbed into him. Joshua's focus narrowed to the thick digit sliding in and out of his ass, the way his passage clamped down on the invading finger, trying to pull it farther into his body. Then there was another sliding alongside the first. "Thank you, Sir," Joshua grunted. His body trembled, and sweat rolled down from his temple. "Oh, God, Sir…."

Joshua whimpered when Nash pulled his fingers free and then sighed in relief when he felt the sheathed head of Nash's cock pushing against his entrance. Joshua tried to relax as Nash slowly entered him, inch by excruciatingly slow inch, but his body was thrumming with need, clenching and jerking. The burn was hot, and Joshua gasped, damn near unable to pull air into his lungs as it turned into white-hot heat. Joshua's heart stopped beating, and his breath stuck in his lungs as Nash continued to push deep.

"Fuck, fuck, fuck," Nash cursed, buried deep in Joshua's clenching ass. Nash stilled but Joshua could feel the trembling within Nash with the effort it took not to move. "Ah, fuck, Joshua," Nash gasped. "I have to move. Please tell me I can move."

Joshua heard the urgency in Nash's voice but he couldn't speak; the sensation of being full and the burn that was fading to a sweet ache robbed him of his voice. He raised his head and looked over his shoulder, met Nash's black eyes with his own heated gaze, and nodded.

Nash groaned and moved, languidly at first, only pulling out a little before pushing back in deep. "Ah, fuck," he gasped again.

The steady pace didn't last long. It couldn't. Nash grabbed Joshua's shoulders in both his hands, fucked Joshua hard and fast.

His eyes rolled up, heart hammering. "Sir…. Sir, please, Sir!"

A hand slid beneath his body, the ring around Joshua's cock fell away. "Come for me, Joshua. Let me feel you come on me."

"Sir!" Joshua screamed as his orgasm ripped through him. White dots danced behind his eyes. He was still coming, only barely aware of Nash slamming into him one last time and roaring his release. Completely spent, Joshua slumped onto the bench, let it hold him, melted into it. He was floating again and stopped thinking beyond the warm sated feeling surrounding him. With a smile on his face, Joshua closed his eyes. He trusted that Nash would watch over him, care for him, bring him back again.

~*~

Last night I had the most amazing experience in my life. It was like all the fucking stars aligned just perfectly. Nash took me somewhere I've never been, somewhere I hoped was real but was beginning to think was a stupid dream. I'd had glimpses of that kind of peace, wanted it so fucking much but....

It didn't last.

It never does.

I should be happy, over the goddamn moon that I'd finally experienced what I'd been searching my whole miserable life for, and I was for a brief moment.

Then I woke up. Reality came rushing back, the magic of a dream popping like a pin to a balloon.

You see, I'm terrified most of the time. Afraid of what I've done, what I'm doing, or what I may have to do. I'm a junkie—pain and peace are my drugs, yet I thrive on turmoil while craving the peace and desiring the pain. How fucked-up is that?

I've become the one I hated.

I might have been able to draw the fantasy out a bit longer, but I made the mistake of looking in the mirror. I knew better. I avoid looking at my reflection. My self-loathing is so great I fear I'll lunge at my own image.

Shattered glass.

Cut myself.

Blood flowing.

Love, hope, freedom lost.

Today I must play my role again. The perfect sub. Say all the right things. Stand perfectly.

A friend is what Nash told me I needed.

I don't have any friends.

Never have.

Chapter Six

THE DENIM jeans were stiff, the new shoes tight as was the stupid polo shirt. Joshua looked like a poser, and more importantly, he felt like one. It hadn't helped that his "Daddy" had to give him a ride to meet his new little friend for lunch. Jesus H. Christ this was a first. He also had no clue why Nash insisted he had new clothes for his play date. It wasn't only the clothes but the amount he'd spent that was ludicrous. Nash could have saved a shit-ton of money by going to the thrift store, and they would have been far less stiff.

Oh well, nothing Joshua could do about it now as he was standing outside the restaurant. He took a moment to get his irritation under control. He pulled at his new clothes and soothed down his windblown curls with a shaking hand. He was definitely nervous. Why, he wasn't sure. He knew Denny—a little—and he seemed like a nice enough person, but Joshua couldn't shake the nagging feeling that he was somehow being set up. For what, he wasn't sure. There was no reason he could think of, so perhaps it was simply his fucked-up head making shit up. He took a deep breath and tried to look like he wasn't freaking out as he opened the door and made his way inside. The aromas of basil, oregano, garlic, as well as warm yeast from freshly baking bread, one of his favorites, hit him and his nerves eased marginally as his belly growled. He'd barely taken two steps when a hand landed on his wrist, and Denny popped up next to him.

"Joshua, hey, great timing. I just got here myself."

A waiter passed by with a large tray of food. "Have a seat wherever you like."

Joshua scanned the area. All the window seats were taken, as were most of the center tables. "Wow, this place is crazy busy."

"Always is. They have the best pasta in town." Denny went up on tiptoes next to him, apparently looking for something as well. "C'mon. I see one at the back."

Joshua followed him. He had no choice in the matter. It took everything to keep up with Denny as the little man easily dodged and weaved through the narrow passages between the tables. At the back of the room, Denny slid into a booth with his back to the door, allowing Joshua to sit on the opposite side and have a clear view of the room.

Joshua cocked his head and studied a smiling Denny. "How did you know I don't like sitting with my back to the door?"

Denny grinned and shrugged a shoulder. "Took a guess. Figured with your brooding disposition and twitchy nature, you'd be more comfortable when able to see what was happening around you."

"Brooding disposition? Twitchy? How the hell do you know what kind of fucking disposition I have? You don't know me," Joshua said defensively.

"Whoa there, hotty man. I meant no disrespect." Denny held up his hands as if to ward off an attack. "I'm a sub. It's in my nature to pay attention to others around me. I've seen you at the club. You seem to always be frowning, even when you try to smile." He nodded toward Joshua's hands. "Your knuckles are white, shoulders tight, and you keep blinking."

Joshua unclasped his hands and shook them. "Sorry I snapped at you. This whole thing of meeting for lunch and making small talk with someone is kind of new for me."

"Dude, that has got to be the saddest thing I've ever heard."

Denny's sincerity caused Joshua to bristle again. "Don't pity me."

"I don't," Denny insisted. "Want me to give you a shoulder massage? It might help with some of the tension."

Denny started to rise, but Joshua stopped him with a gesture of his hands. "No, that's quite all right. I'll be fin... I mean, I'm good." He rolled his neck, the tension causing it to snap and pop. "Besides, I'm not sure the patronage would appreciate it."

"Ain't that the truth." Denny winked. "If I got my hands on you, I'm sure it wouldn't have a family-friendly rating."

"You're quite the little tease, aren't you?"

"Part of my charm." Denny batted his long lashes at Joshua.

Joshua wasn't the least bit impressed, nor was he flattered by Denny's wanton behavior. "At least you have that," he snapped, then instantly felt guilty when Denny's face fell. This was Joshua's issue, and despite his discomfort with the idea, he had no right to take it out on Denny. "Hey, I didn't mean that. I'm a bit shaken, but I shouldn't be taking it out on you. You're right. I am twitchy, because, honestly, I'm not sure why I'm here."

"You mean besides the food and all?"

Joshua looked at Denny and sighed. "Yeah, besides that."

"Well, from what Master Malcolm has told me, you don't have a lot of friends here, you being from out of town and all. He thought you and I might get along." Denny smiled. "I kind of like the idea. I am friendly with some of the guys at the club, but I really don't have that many… actually, I don't have any close friends. I'm a bit flighty and tend to get on people's nerves after a while." Denny looked at him for a long moment, his eyes serious and his mouth set in a straight line. Then he suddenly beamed and laughed, a delighted sound that could have been infectious if Joshua hadn't been so tense. "Anyway, we really are quite the interesting pair."

"Aren't we, though? You're flighty, I'm twitchy. I'm brooding, and you're a pain in the ass." Joshua leaned back and grinned. "Sounds like the perfect recipe for world domination."

"Only if you take the lead. I'll forget the plan an hour from now."

Denny smiled and bounced in his seat as he played with his napkin, his clothes, his hair, and the salt and pepper shakers. In constant motion. Joshua could see how that could wear on someone's nerves after a while. Denny didn't seem aware he was being scrutinized. His eyes, like his hands, were everywhere.

Finally, Denny appeared to calm. He cocked his head, reminiscent of a puppy, and stared at Joshua for a few motionless seconds. "Umm, you have a problem with topping—I mean, leading?"

"Leading, no. Topping?" Joshua grinned slyly. "That depends on who it is bending over for me."

Denny literally started to vibrate, and the bouncing intensified.

Joshua couldn't help but laugh. "Simmer down, Flighty. Hate to burst your bubble, but I have a contract that says I can't dip my dick in anything or have a dick dipped in me without prior written consent by the big man in charge."

Denny pouted and stopped moving long enough to take a sip of his water. "Damn, that's too bad. I don't have the same kind of restriction, so if you ever want to get a little naughty and break some rules…." He tilted his head again, leaving the offer hanging in the air. "Well, you know?"

"I'll keep that in mind, but I wouldn't hold my breath if I were you. I can't do shit without asking Nash for permission first…." Something nagged at him, something Denny had said a moment ago. "Wait, what do you mean you don't have the same kind of restrictions? Nash referred to you as Malcolm's boy?"

"Only a temporary situation. It's not official or anything." Denny waved a dismissive hand. "Malcolm's a good man. He's taken me in hand to try to help me with some of my issues. I've never been contracted, too hard for me to stay focused on anyone or anything for too long." Denny shrugged one shoulder and went back to playing with the salt and pepper shakers. "It makes it hard to do what you're told when your brain misfires all the time and you forget what you're supposed to be doing."

"I sort of envy you. You don't have to worry about him having to know where you are and what you're doing twenty-four seven. You can tell him to fuck off if he tells you to jump, and call him out on his bullshit."

Denny gasped, and Joshua looked up to see the shock evident in his blue eyes.

"Ignore me. I'm in a mood today, and well, I wonder if submitting is all it's cracked up to be some days." *Especially when he keeps forcing up shit from the past*. Shit Joshua didn't want to think about. Ever. He gave himself an internal shake. He didn't want that fucked-up mess ruining his lunch. It wasn't Denny's fault, and Joshua wasn't in the mood to try to swallow down bile. It would only ruin his meal.

"I get it. Submitting can be difficult, and freedom hard to give up. I'll give you that." Denny sighed. "But I think if you find someone who cares enough about you, who wants the best for you, who protects you, that you'll give up control of your free time." Denny leaned over the table and stared at him. "It's worth it. Don't you think?"

Sometimes it is, and other times it will mess you up and make you think of past shit that will fucking gut you. Joshua leaned across the table, mimicking Denny, and stared right back. "Most days, but…." He sat back into the booth and laughed bitterly. "Like I said, ignore me. I'm the twitchy brooding type, remember."

"How about we work on putting you in a better mood? Let's order some food. Have a drink or two if you like. It's on me."

"I don't drink, but thanks anyway."

"Then have tea," Denny said. He waved a waitress over. "Could I get a glass of iced sweet tea and my friend will have…."

"I'll have water with lemon, please."

The tiny brown-haired girl, who barely looked old enough to have a job, nodded and smiled shyly. "And do you need a moment longer before you're ready to order?"

"I know what I want." Denny looked at Joshua. "Do you need a minute?"

Joshua grabbed a menu from the holder. "Umm, what do you recommend?"

"The best chicken alfredo in town," Denny said confidently.

Joshua glanced at Denny and then back at the waitress. "I'll just have what he's having." The girl nodded and hurried off.

"I don't drink either," Denny stated.

"How come?"

The question was casual, but there was a slight change in Denny's posture. He was suddenly intent, like he wasn't going to treat this as a big joke. A serious Denny was like another creature entirely, yet the change was subtle. "Alcohol is as dangerous as any other drug." Denny shrugged. "It impairs one's judgment," he said with a grin, "and I have enough issues with bad judgment without it. You?"

His reasons were simple, and he didn't mind discussing them. "You know that brooding disposition you were talking about?"

"Yeah?"

"It intensifies tenfold."

"Oh dear Lord." Denny's eyes went comically wide. He then blew out a breath and shook a single finger at Joshua. "No alcohol for you, hotty man."

The waitress appeared with a tray laden with dishes. Pasta, bread, salad—plates filled the table in short order, and Denny looked at it and beamed. Actually fucking beamed. Obviously, the man was a major foodie if he got a boner from his dinner being served.

"Oh. My. God. This looks and smells amazing."

"This smells like we'll be able to ward off vampires for a hundred-mile radius," Joshua remarked.

"And that's a bad thing?" Denny winked.

"No, an evening without encountering the Prince of Darkness isn't a bad thing," Joshua insisted, picking up his fork.

"Dude! You're not a fan of Ozzy?"

Joshua stared at Denny, unblinking. Then it hit him, and he started laughing. Denny joined in, and the sound filled Joshua with warmth. He'd been so frickin' nervous about this "date," but he was beginning to realize he'd been silly to worry. Denny was on the same level Joshua was. Two subs trying to find their way. He didn't have to worry about his posture, what he said, or keeping his eyes lowered. It felt good to have someone to cut up and joke with, if only for a little while. Plus he liked the Prince of Darkness, Ozzy Osbourne. The guy couldn't be all bad.

Joshua took a bite of his pasta, the flavor of garlic exploding across his taste buds. Alfredo wasn't his favorite, but it wasn't bad, and there was the added bonus of the vampire repellent thingy.

He washed down his food with a sip of water, then asked, "You said Malcolm was taking you to hand. There are lots of Doms at the club. Why him?"

"Like I said, I've had a rough time finding a Dom. I've had a couple of bad experiences in a row, and I had honestly given up on finding one who suited me, let alone one that could deal with my issues. I've been through almost everyone at the club. So, when Malcolm offered to take me on, I jumped at the chance. I think he just felt sorry for me."

"I couldn't stand to be with someone who felt that way. I hate being pitied," Joshua said with true conviction. No way could he handle it. He fucking hated it when Nash looked at him with a sympathetic expression. Hated it!

"I don't mind. I'm just lucky he was willing to help. Plus, he's like the top of the tops, ya know? It also doesn't hurt that he's super fucking sexy either."

"He is that," Joshua agreed. "I've always had a boner for the older daddies."

"Oh. My. God. Me too! I nearly came in my pants the night he offered to take me in the back. Hell, maybe I did—part of it is a blur—but he beat me and fucked me like I'd never been before. What really blew me away was how quickly I was able to let go and hand over the reins of control to him. Frightening, really. I have trust issues too, by the way. So it even shocked me when he offered to make me his boy until I found the right one for me, and I didn't even hesitate to say yes."

Denny's words were filled with hope, but Joshua caught the hint of sadness in his tone. "But?"

"I have never felt so connected to someone before like I do with Malcolm. And now that I have it…." Denny poked at some pasta, shook his head, and went silent.

"You don't want to give him up?"

"No, but I don't know how I could ever be good enough for him. I mean, he's a god, and I'm"—Denny looked up at Joshua and give him a sad smile—"me."

"Hey, don't sell yourself short. I seriously doubt Malcolm would have agreed to take you on if he didn't see something in you."

Denny didn't respond right away. He ate his meal, but Joshua couldn't help but think Denny's mind was on what Joshua had said, not his food.

After a couple of minutes, Denny nodded and said, "Yeah, I guess so." Denny took another bite and lifted his glass. "What about you? What does Nash see in you?"

I have no fucking clue, was the first thing that popped in Joshua's head. Surprisingly, he was enjoying his lunch with Denny and didn't want to put a damper on it by getting too deep into his issues.

He decided to go with a version of the truth. "To be honest, we are still working things out. We're both really different people with different needs…. Well, on some things. For now, I do for him, he takes care of me. It's tit for tat. We haven't really gotten into the deeper stuff yet."

"Sounds like we're both in sort of a transition period."

The story of my life. He was always in transition or some shit where he had to learn to deal with battling wants and desires.

"Can I ask you something?"

"Sure. I can't promise I'll answer, but you can ask," Joshua said. He tried to sound nonchalant, but his tone was sad even to his own ears.

"There are some rumors running rampant in the club. They say you can handle more pain than all the subs combined."

Joshua, uncomfortable with this line of conversation, wasn't sure how to respond. Although he barely knew Denny, it felt wrong to outright lie to him. Then again, he wasn't sure if the full truth was any of his business.

He took a sip of water, then responded over the rim. "Rumors sometimes have a small sliver of truth, but usually are exaggerated and blown out of proportion."

Denny licked a drop of sauce from his finger, then raised his brows. "And?"

"And I guess I can handle a lot of pain, but I highly doubt I can handle more than all the subs combined."

"Conrad told me he overheard Kirk say you scared the shit out of him. Is that one of those exaggerations too?" Denny asked, but he was looking at his plate, not at Joshua.

"I know that's your way of beating around asking me if I'm a slut for pain, and yeah, I guess I am. But aren't we all to some degree or another? I mean, Malcolm's range is legendary. I've never played with him, but I hear tears come quickly with him."

"You have a point, and yeah, they do." Denny giggled.

"Okay, my turn to ask you a question. You ever play with Nash?"

"Yeah, several times. He's not as hard-core as some of the Doms, but he's fun."

A strange feeling came over Joshua. He wasn't sure what it was. He was pissed and sad. Actually more pissed than sad, but he had no idea why. The emotions coursing through him were foreign, something he'd never experienced before.

Wait. Joshua froze with his fork halfway to his mouth. Holy fuck, he was jealous, which was completely and utterly stupid. He'd never been the possessive type. He wasn't a huge fan of his Dom sharing him with every Tom, Dick, or Harry but hadn't ever had a problem watching his Dom take on another sub. Threesomes, foursomes, and group orgies were hot as hell. Christ, he'd taken himself in hand countless times and blown his load while watching his Dom fuck and beat another sub. He'd also gotten off in a major way the night he was put on stage and a Dom fucked him while another took a crop to his chest, stomach, and dick. He had no idea why he was suddenly feeling the way he was.

"Whoa, did I say something wrong?" Denny asked. He reached across the table and laid his hand on Joshua's forearm, suddenly looking very nervous. "I thought you knew. I mean, I haven't been with him since you two hooked up. Nash hasn't been with any of the boys since he's been with you."

"No, you didn't say anything wrong. Was just thinking about something else," Joshua said in an attempt to lighten the mood. It was just a small fib. One he had to tell because he honestly didn't know how to deal with the shit he was feeling.

"Oh, good. I wouldn't want to upset you."

"Nah, you didn't." A thought occurred to Joshua, and he added, "In fact, you may be able to help me understand him."

Denny patted Joshua's arm, then sat back. He picked up a breadstick and munched on it. "I'll try. What are you having difficulty with?"

"He gave me my own room—"

"Seriously? You lucky bastard. My friend Julian has a pallet next to his master's bed and in two years hasn't slept on a mattress. Seriously, dude, two fucking years. No way could I handle that. I'm a total cuddle whore, but at least you have a bed. And honey, I'd take that and a body pillow over a pallet any day of the week."

Joshua set his fork down, sat back in his chair, and picked at his breadstick, while the man rambled on about beds, cuddling, and all the people he knew who either liked or hated cuddling. It had nothing to do with what Joshua wanted to ask him, and his crazy chatter certainly wasn't going to help with Nash. Joshua didn't dare interrupt. He decided the animated man was quite cute when he was on a roll, and Joshua was enjoying the show immensely.

It took several minutes before Denny realized what he was doing. His cheeks turned a bright shade of red. "I was babbling, wasn't I?"

"Uh-huh. But at least you're cute while doing it."

Denny preened a little at the praise. "Okay, so umm... yeah. I totally forgot what you asked me." Before Joshua could answer, Denny blurted out "Oh, I remember. You were talking about Nash giving you your own room." He bounced in his seat while clapping. "Yay, me!"

"Good job," Joshua praised. He winked then became more serious. "I do appreciate having my own room, but I find I resent him for keeping me out of his." He set the bread down without haven taken a bite. "I know he enjoys me being in his bed, so I don't understand why he's punishing me. I haven't done anything. At least I don't think I have. So any suggestions on how I can get him to stop being a dick and let me in his bed?"

"Oh sweetie, haven't you learned all Doms can be dicks? But in all seriousness, have you asked him what you can do to gain entry into his snuggle world?"

"No, and damn sure not in those words," Joshua answered.

"Fine, use your own words," Denny said flippantly. He munched on his dinner, speaking with his mouth full as he continued. "You're a smart little sub. You said he enjoys you being there. I suggest you make him *need* you there."

"And how am I supposed to do that?"

"Do you have to serve him coffee and breakfast in bed? Malcolm is a tyrant without his morning coffee."

"Yeah, he likes his coffee in bed. I don't think he's a tyrant without it, but he does get a bit grumpy." Joshua laughed.

"So tomorrow take him his coffee a few minutes earlier than he expects it. Instead of going to your knees and waiting for him to wake up to the smell of the fresh brew, slide beneath the covers, wrap your lips around his dick, and blow him awake. He'll open those eyes with a big ol' smile on his face."

Joshua raised an eyebrow, pausing just long enough to say, "And this is getting me in his bed all night, how?" He finished the last bite of his pasta. He set his fork down, surprised he'd cleared his plate.

"I told you it was good." Denny nodded toward Joshua's plate. "Anyway, after a good-morning orgasm, move up and snuggle into his side while he is drinking his coffee. Now, from what I know about Nash, he'll thank you—he's so fucking polite all the time—and want to return the favor."

"Well, I'd never say no to a little reciprocation." Joshua knew he was grinning entirely too widely, even though he still had no idea how this was going to help him get into Nash's bed all night. He was a sucker, literally, for a good pole-slurping, especially when said pole-slurping was being done by a cocky and confident Dom.

"Your job is to make sure he thinks it's his idea, his pleasure that has you using that sexy hot bod of yours for a pillow every night."

"They do like to be the one calling the shots. Okay, so morning blowjobs, what else?"

Denny winked and licked his lips, looking particularly naughty, sort of like a demented sprite. "I'd rather show you."

"Denny," Joshua said warningly.

"Not my fault," he said, sporting an impressive pout. "If you weren't so yummy-looking."

"Thank you, but focus, will you?"

"I'll try." Denny winked. "Okay, so, instead of just blowing him awake, make sure you lube yourself up before you make his coffee. Then, when it's time to get him… up, go down on him like usual, but just before he pops, crawl up his body and sit on his cock."

"Ohhhh," Joshua breathed and felt his own cock react to that suggestion. "Oh, that is wicked."

"Trust me, he will want you in his bed every morning."

"Thank you. You're far more creative than I am."

"Possibly just more of a pervert," Denny said with a wink.

"I seriously doubt that." Joshua grinned.

Denny snorted. "Anyway, walk to heel all the time. Keep your posture perfect, get naked every chance you get. And baby, even if you don't feel it, pretend to be the perfect little sub. It will make him happy. Content. When he's like that, you have a much better chance of reaching your goal of nightly snuggles."

"I've been doing the complete opposite. I mean, I do what he says, but I don't even try to go the extra mile. I think I've been blaming him for being a dick, then trying to figure out a way to get what I want." Joshua grinned. "I kind of like the idea of manipulating him."

"We all use manipulation to some extent. Just don't get content. Trying to use that technique for too long will only come back to bite you in the ass. And not in a good way."

"I'll be sure to keep that in mind. You haven't steered me wrong yet." He pointed to his plate. "That was delicious."

"Glad you liked it," Denny said with another grin. "Let's do this again. I don't have any friends in the scene, and it's nice to have a conversation where I don't have to monitor everything I say." He waved the waitress over.

"Sure, I'd like that." And surprisingly he wasn't lying. He'd been irritated that Nash and Malcolm had set this up and given Joshua no say in the matter. Now, he figured he owed them both a thank-you. He really had enjoyed talking with Denny. It was strange being with someone who didn't want anything from him. Stranger still that Joshua didn't want anything in return. A rare thing in his life.

"I gotta run. I promised Malcolm I'd be back in time to draw his bath. Thanks for having lunch with me, Joshua. Tell Master Nash I said hi." He signed the check and slid his card back into his wallet before going to his feet.

"Will do." Joshua wiped his mouth with his napkin, dropped it on his empty plate, and stood. "Great to meet you and thank you for the advice." He stuck out his hand.

"Not a problem," Denny said, ignoring the offered hand. He wiggled over to Joshua and pulled him into a quick hug. Just as quickly, he spun away and waved over his shoulder. "See you around."

Joshua smiled as he watched Denny sashay away. Yeah, Joshua definitely owed them a thank-you. He couldn't remember the last time he'd had such a great time eating a meal. His smile grew wider as he headed out of the restaurant.

Chapter Seven

NASH WAS going to have to get Malcolm a gift. It was his idea that Joshua and Denny have lunch together, and since Joshua returned from his date, he'd had a smile on his face. It was good seeing his boy happy. Nash had witnessed Joshua's brilliant smile, but to see it from something as simple as a lunch date warmed Nash's heart. However, as nice as it was, Nash couldn't lose sight of his plan. It would do neither of them any good to deviate from it now. Especially since it was still so new. To take even a day, a single hour off, would send the wrong message. Consistency was the key to their success.

Tonight he'd try edging. It would overwhelm Joshua's senses, push him until it all became too much, ending in explosion. Joshua would be left in a state of pure exhaustion both in mind and body. Peace in the aftermath of destruction. In theory anyway. Now, if Nash could keep a tight rein on his own desires long enough to take Joshua to the goal.

Nash took in the playroom, where everything was prepared for the evening. The spanking bench was folded up and tucked away and in its place sat a physician's exam table, modified to suit his needs. The heavy leather cuffs attached to each side as well as the stirrups would scare the bejesus out of most patients. Nash had also attached thick leather straps with buckles along both sides of the table, which could be used to immobilize head, torso, and legs. On the table next to the chair, Nash had laid out lube, condoms, a cock ring, a flogger, small metal clamps with the teeth covered in rubber, and two thin chains. He'd also set out a couple bottles of cold water. Knowing Joshua's abilities to control his responses to stimuli as well as his extraordinary pain tolerance, it could take quite some time to achieve the desired results. Satisfied everything was ready, Nash started to call Joshua down to the playroom, but reconsidered.

Preparing the room, rechecking it, planning the scene, and the anticipation had Nash hard the entire time. If he had Joshua naked and bound before him, there was a very real possibility of it being over before it even got started. Totally unacceptable.

Nash popped the button and lowered the zipper on his jeans, exposing his straining cock. He grabbed the lube and walked across the room to lean against the wall. He poured a small amount of lube in his hand, shoved the tube in his pocket, then wrapped his fist around his dick. He stroked himself from base to tip, twisting his wrist on each upstroke to run his palm over the sensitive cockhead. Keeping his gaze on the chair his boy would soon occupy, Nash reached up with his free hand and pinched his nipple, teasing it as he increased the pressure and speed of his strokes. He worked it harder, faster, the bite of pain in his nipple adding to the eroticism. In no time at all, a knot formed at the base of his spine, balls drawing up tight, readying for release. Nash didn't even try to draw out the pleasure. He arched his back, bit down on his bottom lip to keep from crying out, and filled his hand with warm spunk. One last spurt and he shuddered.

He looked down at the mess in his hand and chuckled. The things he did for his boy. He shook his head at himself. He really should be able to control his urges better. It was for a good cause. Now that he'd released a little pressure, he'd be able to concentrate on Joshua. He supposed he should feel bad, considering what he was about to put Joshua through, but he didn't. It had felt too damn good, and the fact that he was doing it for Joshua's benefit made it all the better. He had nothing to be sorry for. If Joshua weren't so damn sexy…. Still laughing, Nash grabbed some tissues, cleaned up his hand, then tossed the soggy tissues in the trash can. He fastened up his pants and smoothed down his T-shirt, then his hair. After one last look around the room, he was satisfied with his preparation and headed upstairs to get his boy.

Nash found Joshua in the kitchen, wiping down the counters, dressed in nothing but a loose-fitting pair of cotton gym shorts, just as Nash had instructed. Nash stepped up behind Joshua and wrapped his arms around Joshua's waist.

He kissed the warm skin, tasting soap. "How was your shower?"

"It was nice, Sir."

Nash slid his hand beneath the waistband of Joshua's shorts, his fingers brushing along the smooth skin around Joshua's cock. "Mmm, you shaved. I like it."

Joshua pushed back, his firm ass pressing against Nash's groin. Nash continued to skim along Joshua's skin and let his boy grind against him for a couple of minutes.

"Did you have any problems with the enema?" Nash had offered to assist, knowing the process could be a bit of a pain in the... well, anyway, Joshua had declined, but Nash had enjoyed seeing the pink light up Joshua's cheeks. It wasn't often that something so simple could embarrass his boy.

"No, Sir. All clean, shaved, and I even lubed myself up. Just in case you have a use for my clean ass."

"Such a thoughtful boy. Thank you." Nash kissed Joshua's neck again, then released him and stepped back. "Follow me. We're going to the playroom."

Nash turned and headed back down the stairs with Joshua at heel. Once they were behind the closed door, Nash turned to face Joshua. "Remove your shorts and stand next to the table."

Joshua instantly shoved his shorts down and stepped out of them as he moved into position. He kept his eyes respectfully low, but Nash could tell by the way his boy's breath hitched that he was taking in the room and liking what he saw. Maybe it was the flogger that had his attention. Didn't matter, because he was about to get a whole lot more excited.

Joshua stood tall, hands clasped behind his back, chest pushed out, posture perfect. Nash took a moment to appreciate his boy's well-defined body and long slender cock as it strained upward, bobbing with each breath Joshua took. Nash picked up the cock ring, then went to his knees in front of Joshua. Nash ran his tongue along the length of Joshua's cock from the base to the head. He took it into his mouth, scraping his teeth along the sensitive skin and teasing the small slit with the tip of his tongue. The muscles in Joshua's legs tensed, but it was the only response. Nash worked it harder, taking Joshua deep, playing with the heavy balls until he pulled a small sound of pleasure from Joshua. Nash let Joshua slip from his mouth.

He looked up, caught Joshua watching him, and licked his lips. "You taste good." He took Joshua's wet dick in hand and fastened the cock ring snugly around the base. He kissed the head of Joshua's dick, then rolled to his feet. He had to hide his grin when Joshua's bottom lip protruded, no doubt disappointed that the oral play wasn't continuing.

Nash patted Joshua's hip. "On the table."

Joshua did as he was instructed, stretching out, hard dick swaying with each movement. Nash had the sudden urge to take it back into his mouth and drive his boy out of his mind, but he tamped down on his desire. *Slow buildup*, he reminded himself. Instead of giving in to the impulse, he secured Joshua's right wrist to the table and then his left.

"How does that feel? Too tight?"

Joshua opened and closed his hands, then tugged on the restraints. "No, Sir. They feel good."

Nash then moved down to Joshua's feet and secured each ankle with a heavy leather cuff. He tapped one. "How about these? Feel okay?"

"Yes, Sir."

"Very good. For tonight until the end of the scene, you are allowed to speak. You can beg, plead, scream, whatever you want. You may also look at me. In fact, I encourage it as I love seeing the lust in your eyes. Although, considering you're not allowed to come, I may be seeing a little panic and frustration rather than lust. The good news is, that is your only rule. Is that understood?"

Joshua looked down his body. His expression showed his concern, but he nodded. "Yes, Sir."

Nash arched a brow. "Any questions?"

"No, Sir. I'm sure whatever you have in mind, I'll enjoy it." Whether consciously or subconsciously, Joshua thrust his hips, no doubt hoping for a little more lip action. He would have to wait. Nash had other plans at the moment.

Nash picked up the nipple clamps. He bent and sucked first one then the other nub until they were erect. Without warning, Nash quickly attached a clamp to Joshua's right nipple.

"Fuck!" Joshua yelled. His back arched.

Nash gave him a couple of seconds to adjust to the stinging pain. When Joshua eased back against the chair and blew out a breath, Nash instantly attached the other clamp. Joshua cried out again, but this time he settled back much quicker.

Nash flicked one of the clamps. "How does that feel?"

"It fucking hurt like hell, Sir."

"And you love it." It wasn't a question. Nash could tell by the look of bliss on Joshua's face, he'd enjoyed the stinging pain. Nash grinned and randomly jostled the clamps. His smile grew when he got a pleasure-filled sound in response. Only then did Nash pick up the two lengths of silver chains. He attached each end of the shorter chain to the clamps, making sure it was taut, then looped the longer one over it, pulled it tight, and attached the end to the cock ring.

Nash stepped back and admired his work. The silver chains looked amazing against Joshua's flushed skin. "Mmm, very nice."

Whatever Joshua was going to say was interrupted by a yelp when Nash tugged on the chain that ran along his stomach. "What was that? I thought you loved the sting?"

"I do, but damn, I wasn't expecting that."

"Shall I quit?"

"Not on my account, Sir."

"You're right. This is about my pleasure and I think it will be my pleasure to continue."

"By all means," Joshua said with a sly grin.

Nash ran the tip of his finger along the cool wood of the flogger and wondered briefly how long it would take before he could wipe that cocky grin off Joshua's face. *Only one way to find out*. He picked up the flogger and ran the soft tails across his palm. Joshua eyed the flogger, his excitement shining in his dark eyes.

"You have your safewords."

"Yes, Sir. Yellow to slow down and red to stop."

"Remember, there is no failure in using your safewords. In fact, I expect you to use them. You are to warn me if you are close to coming. Is that understood, boy?"

"Yes, Sir."

Nash pulled his arm back. "We begin." He let his arm fly, the tips of the flogger hitting just above Joshua's right pec. Nash worked the flogger in a figure-eight pattern, being mindful not to hit the clamps. Instead, he worked his way down Joshua's right side from shoulder to toes before doing the same on his left side in the opposite pattern. Nash kept his strokes steady, his swing measured. Before long, Joshua's skin turned a lovely shade of pink. Nash's strikes weren't forceful enough to cause pain; that would come from the sheer repetition of strokes. Other than the tone of Joshua's skin, there were no further indications that Joshua felt the blows. Nash switched hands, followed the same path but with marginally more power to his strikes.

It took several more passes around Joshua's body before Nash got a true response. A well-placed slap to Joshua's inner thigh caused him to arch, his hands curling into tight fists. He tensed briefly but settled down quickly. Soon, he wouldn't be able to relax so easily. Nash was determined.

Joshua's restraint and tolerance to pain were amazing, but he couldn't hide his arousal. Sweat beaded on his brow, his lips were parted, and his hard cock wept. His body moved with each blow in an erotic dance. Although Nash had only recently gotten off, his cock hardened. How could it not? The sight of Joshua, the sound of the flogger against his skin, the soft grunts and moans he was making were heady.

Now that Joshua's skin was heated and he was making wonderful rousing sounds that filled the room, Nash showed his appreciation by concentrating the blows on Joshua's torso, inching closer and closer to the clamps, knowing Joshua would appreciate the flare of pain and add to his pleasure. Joshua was literally thrumming—proof his anticipation was hard to contain. With a flick of Nash's wrist, the tips of the flogger landed on the first one then the other nipple in rapid succession.

"Oh God." Joshua moaned, a pure guttural sound.

Nash continued to let the flogger fly, keeping a critical eye on Joshua's skin. His boy might be able to handle the pain, but Nash had no desire to cause any serious harm. Joshua groaned when Nash directed his blows lower. He positioned himself at Joshua's hip and found a rhythm working the flogger across Joshua's chest, down his stomach to lightly lay the tails of the flogger to Joshua's cock and balls.

"Oh. Fuck. Yes!" Joshua cried out, body going bowstring tight.

Nash concentrated on Joshua's groin until his boy was panting and dancing beneath the flogger. Each movement caused the chains to tug on the clamps. The area around Joshua's nipples turned an angry red, yet Joshua continued to beg for more with his sounds and body. Nash allowed it a little longer. Joshua's tolerance for pain was insane, the way he craved and begged for it even more so. As evident by the scars upon Joshua's body, he didn't worry about permanent damage. Nash did. He gradually lessened the strength of his blows until they were barely brushing Joshua's skin.

"Please, don't stop," Joshua begged.

"We are just getting started, boy," Nash assured him. He dropped the flogger, and it hit the floor with a thud.

Joshua's eyes flew open, and he met Nash's gaze with a pleading expression. "Please," he whimpered.

"Are you close?"

Joshua shook his head. "Not yet. Feels good, but…." He swallowed hard.

"But what?"

"I could be if you picked that flogger back up and swung a little harder, faster."

Nash cocked his head. "Boy, are you trying to tell me how my scene should go? Is this not about my pleasure? My needs?"

"No… I mean, yes, this is about your pleasure, and no, I'm not trying…." Joshua blew out a heavy breath. "Your pleasure is all that matters."

"Yes it is, and I'm thoroughly enjoying myself." Nash beamed.

He adjusted the stirrups to spread Joshua's legs wide, then stepped between them. Joshua's heavy sac was snug against the padded seat, looking mouthwateringly good. A delight that would have to wait. Nash ran his hands over the hot, reddened skin of Joshua's thighs, enjoying the heat against his palms for a moment. Joshua watched him, an expression of wonder on his handsome face as Nash removed the chain from the cock ring. He let it drag across Joshua's chest—he shuddered—as Nash carefully detached it from the clamps and tossed it aside. Nash then laid his hands on Joshua's stomach, running his fingers over the hard ridges of muscles. Joshua moaned louder, eyes once again squeezed shut, body in constant motion. His boy was so incredibly sexy when he gave in to his pleasure.

Before long, Joshua's sounds died down, and his movements calmed, Nash's touch obviously no longer producing the sparks of pain Joshua craved. Joshua's brow furrowed, and he pushed his chest up, no doubt searching for the harder friction. Nash eased his fingertips closer and closer to Joshua's nipples, then in one quick movement, removed both clamps.

The blood rushing back into the abused nipples caused Joshua to scream, the sound echoing off the walls of the small room. He fought against his restraints, but they held, the only thing keeping Joshua on the table. Nash laid his palms on the erect nubs, massaging, fingers digging in a little, kneading the firm muscles, rewarded with another roaring sound. He drew out Joshua's response as long as possible. Nash couldn't take his attention from Joshua's face as he rode the high the pain produced. He was so stunning, and Nash's dick twitched in appreciation.

"Close," Joshua gritted out.

"Deep breaths," Nash instructed, stopping all movement but not removing his hands from Joshua's flesh. It took several deep breaths before Joshua seemed to calm. Nash picked up the lube and squeezed a small amount onto his palm. He rubbed his hands together, warming the gel before wrapping a fist around Joshua's hard cock, and grabbed Joshua's balls with his other hand. Nash set a slow but firm rhythm up and down Joshua's shaft while leisurely flexing his fingers around the delicate sac.

"You respond beautifully to pain. Now let's test your tolerance to simple pleasure."

"Nothing you're doing to me is simple," Joshua groaned. "God, I ache."

"You ache because I desire it," Nash said quietly as he continued to stroke Joshua. "I love it when you ache for me. Going to work you until you ache so fucking bad you beg."

It was extremely important that he teach Joshua the difference in the two sensations. Pleasure in pain didn't need to be achieved through abraded skin or creating welts. No blood needed to flow, no scars, no abuse was required to achieve the high desired. Nash slid his hand from Joshua's balls to his thigh, steadying himself, and pumped Joshua's shaft rapidly from base to tip, using a good amount of pressure. The muscles in his arm screamed, exhaustion setting into them, but he ignored it, worked past the discomfort. A lesson to be taught and learned was more important.

A few more hard pulls on his dick and Joshua cried out. "Yellow. Going to…. Oh. God. Oh. God."

Nash instantly slowed, keeping his fingers loosely around the shaft.

Joshua held his breath, eyes closed tightly. His dick twitched in Nash's hand. Sweat trickled down his temples.

"Deep breaths," Nash encouraged.

Joshua let out a breath slowly, his body tense, trembling, and slick with perspiration. Nash was starting to think Joshua had waited too long, that he wouldn't be able to stave off his impending release. But to Nash's relief and great delight, Joshua finally opened his eyes and swallowed hard. "Whew, that was close, Sir."

"Better now?"

Joshua shifted and blew out a long, drawn-out breath, then nodded. "Yes, Sir."

"Good." Nash went right back to stroking Joshua hard and fast.

It only took a couple of minutes before Joshua screamed again, only this time it was "Red!" Nash instantly dropped his hands to his sides but apparently the loss of sensation hadn't registered yet as Joshua continued to scream, "Red! Red! For fuck's sake, red!"

"I've stopped. Deep breaths. C'mon, boy, you can do it."

Joshua panted harshly, entire body shaking violently, his eyes still squeezed shut.

"C'mon boy, open your eyes. Focus on me, on my voice, not your dick. This is about me, about my needs, not yours." Nash kept his voice low and even, using encouraging words until Joshua once again relaxed against the table. His body trembled, but his breaths were less harsh, and he opened his eyes.

"Good, boy," Nash praised. "Maybe you should keep your eyes open. You seem to cry out whenever you keep them closed too long."

"Wow! I have no idea how I didn't blow. That was fucking intense, Sir. But I'm pretty sure it had nothing to do with my eyes and everything to do with the way you are working my dick."

"Either way, I'm proud of you. That was quite impressive."

"Thank you, Sir," Joshua said. He beamed with the praise, all his cocky swagger absent.

"Would you like some water?"

"Yes, Sir."

Nash brought the table to an upright position. He grabbed a bottle of water, opened it, and placed it against Joshua's lips. He drank down a good amount. "Thank you, Sir."

"Need more?"

Joshua shook his head.

Nash tipped up the bottle and drank down the rest in one long gulp. He recapped it, then tossed it in the garbage can. It hit the rim, then clanked to the ground.

"It's a good thing I'm a much better Dom than a basketball player, huh?" Nash chuckled.

"Very good thing for me, Sir."

"I'm so glad you feel that way. Now back to what I'm good at." He wrapped his hand around Joshua's prick. His boy's eyes went wide.

Chapter Eight

JOSHUA WAS going to shake apart, just fucking shatter into a million little pieces. Nash had spent the last hour bringing Joshua to the edge, but each time Joshua started to take a step over it, Nash would jerk him back, refusing to let him fall into the bliss he sought. Joshua didn't know how much more he could take. He was supposed to be focusing on Nash, but with the way his balls were aching, he was having a difficult time. His overly sensitive cockhead demanded his attention each time Nash came near it, even with the softest of touches. Red was on the tip of his tongue. He was really, really trying to please Nash, but Christ, how much longer was the bastard going to draw it out? Oh, and Nash was truly a bastard. A sadistic one. The smile on his face each time Joshua cried out was proof of just how much Nash was enjoying Joshua's torment.

"You've done so well, you deserve a reward," Nash informed him.

Joshua narrowed his eyes, skeptical. "What kind of reward, Sir?"

"The kind that makes me deliriously happy," Nash said cryptically. He retrieved two heavy chains attached to sheepskin-lined leather cuffs from the cabinet. He attached the end of each chain to a hook in the ceiling. "Scooch your ass to the edge of the table."

Joshua did as he was told and Nash secured the cuffs around Joshua's calves, putting him in the perfect position for fucking, knees spread, ass exposed. At least that's what he hoped was coming next. Nash picked up the condom. Joshua couldn't help but grin, knowing he was getting what he wanted. Hopefully, it wasn't him that would be coming, at least not until Nash allowed it. However, with as worked up as Joshua was, he no longer had confidence in his abilities to follow the rules. Hell, he could barely put a complete sentence together. He was so fucking horny, if he didn't get off soon, his goddamn head was going to explode—both of them.

Nash, however, didn't seem to have the same sense of urgency. He took his dear sweet time unfastening his pants and pulling off his shirt before opening the condom package. Briefly, Joshua was able to concentrate on something other than his own dick as he took some time to admire his Dom's impressive body. The perfect amount of hair across his torso, dark erect nipples, and bulging muscles. From the way his chest was rising and falling, he wasn't as unaffected as he tried to portray. His impressive cock was also straining upward as he rolled the condom on.

Joshua shifted, lifting his ass and thrusting his hips in a wanton attempt to get Nash to hurry up.

"I have an eager boy, I see."

Joshua gritted his teeth at Nash's teasing tone. "Completely your fault, Sir. You're driving me mad."

Nash tilted his head, then ran the tip of his index finger across the tip of Joshua's cock. "That's because you're focusing on this instead of me."

"Hard not to," Joshua snapped.

Nash scowled. "Tone, boy."

Joshua swallowed down his irritation. "Sorry, Sir, it's just…." He pursed his lips. "There is no excuse for my disrespect."

"Apology accepted. Now, I need for you to trust that I know what you can handle. What you need."

Joshua wasn't so sure of Nash's ideas of what Joshua could or couldn't handle. He'd already been reduced to a trembling, babbling fool. Pushed much further and he'd be stark raving mad. He didn't say any of it out loud. It would only slow Nash down because he'd have to give reasons why he deserved trust.

Instead, Joshua said, "Yes, I'm sure you know what I need, Sir."

"Yes, I do." Nash lowered the back of the table until Joshua was lying flat.

Nash took his cock in hand and guided it to Joshua's ass. "Open for me, boy."

"Yes, Sir."

Nash nudged his cockhead against Joshua's hole, but it had been a while since he'd lubed himself up, and with the tension that had settled into his muscles, he was having a hard time relaxing.

Nash pushed again, a little harder this time. "Open yourself, boy."

"Yes, Sir." Saying it and doing it were two completely different things. His body simply wasn't responding to the command.

Nash was persistent, pushing, nudging, and when Joshua still didn't relax, Nash thrust his hips hard, breaching Joshua's ass and going balls deep.

"Jesus!" Joshua arched, the burn intense, robbing him of his ability to breathe.

Nash pulled all the way out and slammed into him again. This time Joshua didn't even have enough air in his lungs to cry out. He could only grit his teeth and ride the pain. It consumed him and freed him. He hated the way his muscles tightened and cramped, but it was necessary to propel him to a higher state of being. He took the pain, processed it, turned it into something different, something he could relate to, and then it happened. He was fucking flying. Nash did know what he needed. The rush was incredible, and it sent him even higher. He was no longer focusing on his dick or any other part of his body, but soaring on a pain-fueled flight of pure bliss.

Nash rode him hard and fast, yet Joshua was able to remove himself from the here and now as if he were floating above his body—aware of what was happening physically, yet not truly reacting to it. That was until Nash took Joshua's cock in hand and stroked it with the same fast and hard rhythm that he was driving in and out of Joshua's ass. It was only then that Joshua sensed the knot coiling within in his balls as he slammed back into his body. The flight was over and just like that, he was on the verge of coming.

"Red! Sir! Sir! Please! Red!"

All movement stopped, but Joshua was so wrapped up in the needs of his body that he heard nothing. Saw nothing. All his senses were stripped, except the heaviness in his sac and the tingling in his cock. He had to come. God, how he needed to come. All he had to do was release the reins he had around his willpower and let it all go. Just step right over the edge and consequences be damned. But, even as he thought it, there was a part of him, the part that wanted to please Nash, that wasn't getting the message. He teetered back and forth in a mental game of tug-of-war. The good thing, or maybe the worst thing, was as the battle went on, the sudden urge to come dissipated and it released its tight hold.

"Are you okay? C'mon, boy. Open your eyes."

Joshua did as he was told and blinked at Nash. He had a concerned expression on his face. "I'm… okay." His voice was hoarse.

"Damn, you scared me. I wasn't sure if you had fallen asleep or passed out."

"Just zoned out for a minute." Joshua shook his head and whistled. "Wow, now that was a fucking rush."

Nash's brows stitched together, no doubt in an attempt to look stern, but he couldn't hide the way his top lip curled at the corner. "I'm glad you're enjoying my pleasure so much."

"Actually, Sir, I'm kind of having a love-hate relationship with your tactics. And to be completely honest, you plow into me again and I don't know if it will matter if I know my safeword."

"Well, let's test that theory, shall we?"

A pitiful-sounding whimper escaped Joshua before he could clamp down on it. He wasn't sure of what was up or down, his mind and body so exhausted, yet he still vibrated with excitement and need. Such a strange sensation, like nothing he'd ever experienced before. This time when Nash entered him there was no pain, but the tingling sensation exploded, and after just two thrusts of Nash's hips, Joshua was once again standing on the brink of detonation.

Red! Red! Red! his mind screamed, yet he was unable to speak. He couldn't get his mouth to work, nor did he have any control over his body. A glut of pleasure.

Then, without warning the tight band was released from his dick. He thought he heard Nash say something, but he wasn't sure what it was or if he had even spoken. He was falling. He'd stepped over the edge and was descending into the abyss. There was no sight, no sound, no smells, just complete and utter peace.

Blackness inched in around his vision. He tried to blink it away, to fight it, but it was as if he were an ethereal being trying to catch smoke. There was no way to combat it, and the blackness closed in until there was nothing.

NASH RELEASED the cock ring. "Come for me." Before he could even finish the sentence, Joshua was coming. Nash wasn't even sure if his boy had heard him. Nash clamped down on his own need, riding out Joshua's release as pulse after pulse landed on Joshua's stomach and chest. It was a herculean effort considering the sight of Joshua in the throes of bliss. His face was slack with pleasure, head tipped back, lips parted in a silent scream. He was so beautiful. His boy. His Joshua.

The last drop seeped from Joshua and only then did Nash give in to his own need. His knees nearly buckled and he fell forward and held his boy's sweat-soaked body. Nash clung to Joshua, listening to the rapid beat of his heart, content and warm. Nash wanted to close his eyes, rest against Joshua's warm skin, sleep. Nevertheless, he couldn't. He had to take care of his boy. Next time, he'd plan better. Make sure they were both in a position to hold each other and bask in the glow of postfuck bliss. With a groan, he lifted up, his dick slipping from Joshua. Joshua didn't move, his breathing slow and even, eyes closed, and a slight smile on his face.

Nash disposed of the condom, then fastened up his pants. A small snuffling sound was the only response from Joshua. Nash smiled at his sleeping boy, went to the bathroom and ran a washcloth under warm water then added a little soap. Before leaving the bathroom, he tossed a towel over his shoulder. He ran the soft cloth across Joshua's chest. He critically checked every inch of visible flesh, satisfied when he found no welts or broken skin. He washed the rest of him and Joshua didn't move, but the small smile never faltered. Nash wondered if his boy was dreaming or if it was simply the remnants of what Nash had done to him. Nash hoped it was the latter but would be totally happy if it were the former as well.

After Joshua was clean and dried, Nash tried to rouse him, but Joshua only grunted. There was no way in hell Nash would be able to carry Joshua upstairs, and apparently, Joshua had no plan of making it on his own. Nash did the next best thing. He rushed up the stairs, grabbed as many pillows and blankets as he could carry, and raced back to the playroom. He created a pallet on the floor, then slid his arms beneath Joshua and lifted him out of the chair.

"Christ, you're heavy," Nash groaned under the weight of his boy.

Joshua—bless his heart—wrapped his arms around Nash's neck and buried his face. It was a damn good thing he only had a few steps to go because he barely made it to the blanket without dropping Joshua. He laid him down, then curled up next to him and pulled the covers over them. Nash couldn't help but feel a bit cocky. The scene had gone better than he'd expected. He'd inflicted no severe pain, hadn't left a single lasting mark, yet he'd pushed Joshua to a beautiful headspace and made him fly. He had no crazy notions that he'd cured his boy of seeking the deeper pain, but it was a step in the right direction. It gave him hope, and with it, Nash had no doubt he and Joshua would make it through their contract and beyond. Nash would never give up until his boy was whole and healthy.

~*~

I'm slowly giving up.

Something bad is going to happen. I just know it. I can feel the dread hanging over me like a dark winter night. Things have been going too well. I'm becoming comfortable, content, happy. I remember this feeling, experienced it several times when I was a child, but every time it ended in a new home, new rules, despair. I want so much to believe this time is different, but history has a way of repeating itself. I know this all too well.

I thought about calling Dr. Hobson and asking him about it. I even thought maybe I could share it with Nash, but in the end, I didn't tell either of them. I'm scared, a fucking coward.

I'm not ready for it to end yet.

Last night Nash sent me to places I didn't believe existed. When I woke this morning, he was right there, wrapped around me like a warm blanket, holding me. He didn't order me to get his coffee and breakfast. When I asked him about them, he said he wasn't ready for us to get up. Us! I like that word. Before getting up, he made love to me. At least that's what I'm calling it. I've never had anyone take me so slowly, so gently. It was a mutual pleasure. We were equals. No rush, no pain, no using my body for their own needs. But, now as I write this, I know it's just my messed-up head making things up. No one makes love to fucked-up people like me. They fuck me, use me, and when they tire of me, toss me away.

Eventually Nash will too.

Happiness always ends.

Always.

Chapter Nine

NASH WAS pacing back and forth in the hallway when Joshua stepped out of the bathroom. "Living room. Now," Nash demanded.

Joshua frowned, then headed for the living room and went right to his knees.

Nash circled him like he was prey, which considering what Nash was about to do him, he supposed he was. They'd had an amazing scene the night before last. Joshua had woken, and Nash swore he'd never seen him so happy, but as the day went on, he became brooding. This morning was no different, and Nash was about to cure him of his damn grumpiness.

"So, what shall I do with you, boy?"

"I'm not sure, Sir," Joshua said quickly. He frowned. "Did I do something to make you mad?"

"No, quite the opposite," Nash replied, walking around him again. "But I did notice how you kept shaking your ass each time you walked by me. You did that on purpose, didn't you?"

"I didn't think I was doing anything on purpose, Sir. I was simply doing my chores. I mean, yeah, I guess I can see how you could take it that way, but I was merely dusting and vacuuming. I can't think of anything…." Joshua bit his lip, effectively stopping the flow of words.

"Hmm, I'm not so sure." Nash stopped in front of Joshua, knowing full well that he was getting an eyeful. "I'm quite sure when you were cleaning the kitchen floor that you were pushing that sweet butt of yours out farther. Am I correct?"

"I didn't think I was, Sir. I was thinking more about…." Joshua sighed. "Nothing really."

Nash decided to relent a little on his pissed-off routine. "Do you like knowing it turns me on to watch you working around the house?"

"Yes, Sir. I always like it when you're turned on "

"Did you have any idea of what you were doing to me? Seeing you on your knees, your ass on display. Do you have any idea what was going through my mind?" Nash rubbed himself through his jean right in front of Joshua's eyes. "You got me so hard from wanting you, I ached."

Joshua's breath caught as he was about to speak. He seemed delightfully distracted by the way Nash was fondling himself and licked his lips before continuing. "No, I didn't realize I was causing you such discomfort, Sir. You should have told me. I would have"— he licked his bottom lip again, this time slowly, sensually—"taken care of it for you."

Nash undid his button and eased the zipper down. "I can't stop thinking how you looked the other night when I fucked you senseless, then seeing you on your knees today? Mmm." Nash moaned, pulling his cock out and stroking it. "A nice spanking, I think, for being a naughty boy would be in order. But right now, I think I'd rather have you sucking me off."

"My pleasure, Sir." Joshua reached forward and took Nash's cock firmly in his fingers, pushing Nash's hand out of the way. He moved closer on his knees and ran his tongue over the head. "It is my duty, after all, to service you."

Nash started to speak, but just then, Joshua swallowed Nash's aching shaft into his throat and speaking no longer seemed all that important. Instead he moaned his appreciation. It felt so damn good. Joshua's mouth was wet and hot, his throat welcoming. "God, yes," Nash whispered, his hips rocking. "That's it. Suck me, boy."

Joshua reached up, took hold of Nash's hips, and sucked eagerly. He made enthusiastic sounds, and his tongue was doing wonderfully creative things to Nash's dick.

Nash looked down at his submissive, on his knees, lips wrapped around Nash's throbbing prick. He enjoyed the sight of Joshua lapping a drop of fluid from the head. "Not going to last long, I'm afraid," Nash said with real regret.

Joshua slid his fingers down Nash's cock and circled the base of his shaft tightly with finger and thumb, effectively ringing him. Then he opened his mouth wider and took Nash deep into his throat, followed by several shallow strokes before swallowing him deep again.

"Oh God!" Nash gasped and thrust. His cock slid between Joshua's lips, and the head slipped into Joshua's throat. Nash shuddered. "Yes," he hissed.

Joshua dropped his hands to his lap, tipped his head back to the perfect angle, and opened his mouth wide. It was all the encouragement Nash needed. He grabbed the back of Joshua's head, curled his fingers in the soft strands of hair, and thrust. Joshua took every inch of him, his tight, wet throat adding the perfect amount of friction. Within minutes he was ready to blow.

"Joshua," Nash whispered. His balls throbbed, and he let go, shoving himself into Joshua's mouth as he came in long pulses. "Oh God, boy." He shook, his legs unsteady, as Joshua sucked him and licked him clean. Joshua apparently noticed Nash's weak state because he got to his feet and helped Nash to the sofa and sat him down. Nash probably should feel embarrassed for his lack of control, but he didn't. He felt too good to worry about such matters at the moment.

"You okay, Sir?" Joshua grinned knowingly.

Nash groaned, his eyes closing. "I'm fine." He lifted his head and smiled when he spotted a drop of come at the corner of Joshua's mouth. Nash pointed at it. "You missed some."

Joshua snaked his tongue out and swiped up the droplet. "Mmm, good to the last drop."

"Good answer." Nash needed a second to compose himself. "Go grab your paddle, boy," he said. The second Joshua turned around, Nash laid his head back once again and took deep, calming breaths.

Nash was breathing much better and the shaking in his legs had lessened when Joshua returned with the heavy, leather-padded paddle with the silver studs. Joshua loved the paddle. Loved the thud it made and how it left him red and sore for a quite some time. It was exactly what Joshua needed. It would give him something other than his brooding thoughts to focus on.

Joshua knelt again and handed over the paddle. "How would you like me, Sir?"

Nash turned the paddle over and over in his hand and pretended to consider it for a moment. "We'll keep it simple, boy. Drop your pants and lie over my lap. And you don't get to come, so don't bother asking. I had to wait all day to get your mouth on me, so you can hold it for a bit."

Joshua stood, popped the button on his jeans, and lowered the zipper slowly, then slid his pants and his briefs down around his thighs.

Nash got a good look at Joshua's erection as it was freed from his briefs. "Tell me, boy. Is that from sucking me or in anticipation of the spanking?"

"Do you want me to be honest?"

"Always," Nash insisted.

"I got a bit of a stiffy when I was blowing you." Joshua grinned and knelt, maneuvering himself over Nash's thighs. "But the thought of the paddle and your heavy hand cranked it up." He was silent for a second then added, "Oh, and because I deserve it for teasing you when I was cleaning, Sir." It was an afterthought, Joshua's own desires prevalent, but at least he'd amended it quickly. He was learning and deserved a reward.

Nash ran a hand over Joshua's ass. "Ready?" Not waiting for a reply, he slapped Joshua's ass hard with the paddle, one hand on Joshua's back to steady him.

Joshua flinched, and his cock pressed into Nash's thigh. "Thank you, Sir."

"You're very welcome, boy." Nash brought his arm down again. He alternated his blows between heavy and light, covering Joshua's ass and raising a healthy glow. Joshua's rock-hard cock slid between Nash's thighs each time the paddle made contact with his ass.

Joshua swayed with each blow, but he didn't beg. A small grunt was the only sound Joshua made. Nash was very aware of the moment when Joshua moved into his subspace. The pain sent Joshua there easier now. Nash wondered briefly if Joshua realized the change, that even a little discomfort could force his concentration and push him deep.

"That's it," Nash said softly, his strokes getting lighter as he slowed and backed off. "Well done." He smoothed a hand over the heated skin of Joshua's ass.

Joshua slid off Nash's thighs and directly to his knees. Nash grinned, noting that he chose to stay up on his knees rather than sit back on his heels. Joshua clasped his hands at the small of his back, lowered his head, and closed his eyes, going silent and still.

Nash leaned back and silently watched as Joshua made the final transitions that allowed him to let go of whatever had been weighing heavily on him.

Finally, when Joshua appeared to be completely calm, his breathing slow and even, Nash cleared his throat. "As much as I like looking at you with your pants shoved down and your cock on display for me, I prefer you naked, boy."

Joshua nodded silently and stood to undress. When he was done, he neatly folded his shirt and pants, then returned to his knees, this time sitting back on his heels. He gasped at the contact then dropped his hands in his lap and lowered his head.

Nash settled in his chair and sighed contently. "You did such a good job I believe you deserve a reward. There's lube and a dildo in the bedside table. Fetch them."

Joshua rolled to his feet, turned, and headed toward the bedroom. Nash took the opportunity to enjoy his handiwork, watching appreciatively as Joshua's reddened ass swayed and flexed with each step. It really was quite the sight to behold, and he felt a twinge of disappointment when Joshua disappeared around the corner. It was brief because soon enough Joshua returned with a sleek, realistic-looking dildo. He went to his knees in front of Nash and held out the toy as well as a battered tube of lube.

"Those aren't for me."

Joshua tilted his head looking confused.

"Give me a show, boy. I want to watch you stroke yourself and play with my toy."

Joshua's prick twitched and strained away from his body stiffly. Joshua scooched back a few feet, set the dildo on the floor, then squeezed a good amount of lube into his palm before setting it down as well. He wrapped his slick fist around his shaft and worked it slowly from base to tip.

"I like the way you're looking at me when I do this." He leaned back, propping himself on one elbow while he continued to stroke his cock at a leisurely pace.

He spread his legs, feet firmly on the floor, and continued to pump himself until he was panting. Nash swallowed hard. The sight of Joshua pleasuring himself was a true treat. Joshua wasn't the only one getting a reward. Nash was enjoying the show immensely.

Joshua spent the next few moments slicking the dildo leisurely, suggestively. Finally, he shifted so he was on his hands and knees. He reached around behind himself, teasing with it at first. He slid it over his hole and pressed it in just enough to stretch.

"Oh, damn…," he breathed just before he arched his back and pressed the dildo deep inside. "So good."

Nash moved to press his hand against his renewed erection. "How does it feel? Is it big enough? Are you feeling the burn?" He pressed again and teased at his zipper.

"It's big," Joshua replied with a growl as he worked the dildo in and out of his body. "Feels good." He swallowed hard. "Fuck yeah. Nice and wide toward the base. Stretches—" His words were cut off by a hiss. He shoved the dildo deep, back arching farther, muscles flexing and rolling. "Burn, but in a good way." He started to move again, riding the dildo, rocking back to meet it, taking it nice and deep with each thrust. "Oh fuck, yes!"

He rode it hard and fast for a bit, his breath coming in short, tight pants until he suddenly went still, frozen midthrust for a moment. He pressed the dildo deep until the wide flat base was flush against his ass then shifted to a sitting position, keeping it shoved to the hilt by his own body weight. He tucked his fingers around his balls and fondled them, rolling them gently in his hand while he caught his breath. "Feels so fucking good when it's this far in me. I can feel my ass clamping down on it, trying to take it in even farther."

"I know just how good that tight ass feels when it's clamped around me," Nash said breathlessly. He slid his zipper down, giving his straining cock a little more room. His prick twitched as he freed it, and he rubbed his palm down the length. "See what you've done to me, boy?" He stroked himself and parted his legs.

Joshua smiled. "I love your cock, Sir. Love that I'm making you hard." He wiggled a bit and moaned. "Love sucking you off." Joshua's fingers moved back to his own erection, and he started to pull at it while he continued to roll and massage his balls with his other hand. "So hot, Sir. Let me suck you. Please, Sir."

Nash slid his fist languidly down his shaft, staring at Joshua's face. His gaze flicked to Joshua's cock, to his ass. "No, I'm going to fuck you," he growled.

"Yes, yes, want you." Joshua's hand sped on his cock, and he rolled his hips, working the dildo in his ass. "Please, Sir, fuck me."

"Then give me a show. Stroke that cock harder, faster."

Joshua instantly obeyed. He pumped his cock, biting his bottom lip, eyes squeezed shut. Fuck, he was gorgeous when giving in to pleasure. Nash clamped his fist tightly around his throbbing cock. "Want to see you come." Nash watched Joshua carefully, seeing the sweat roll down his temples, the rapid rise and fall of his chest, the coiling of his muscles as he got closer and closer. "Now," Nash demanded.

Joshua shot instantly, throwing his head back and shouting his response to the ceiling. He stroked himself; come fountained over his fist until he was spent. He lowered his head, looked down his body, and then his gaze settled on Nash with a satisfied grin on his face. "Oh my. I've made quite the mess haven't I, Sir?" He brought his hand to his mouth and licked his fingers seductively.

Nash growled and jumped to his feet. He pulled a condom from his pocket, opened the packet, and rolled it on. "Hands and knees, boy." The instant Joshua was in position, Nash disposed of the dildo with a twist and pull and slammed himself home, plunging into Joshua's heat.

Joshua grunted, then pressed back wantonly to meet Nash's thrusts. "That's it, fuck me, Sir. Please!"

Nash didn't say anything; he merely grabbed Joshua's hips and pulled him back onto his prick, stabbing into him again and again. Joshua's body clung to him, the scent of sweat and spunk and man all around him. His pulse kicked up, and a tingling sensation raced down his spine, tightened his sac.

"Mine," he roared as he began to come. "My boy." Joshua shivered as Nash came, clenching around him.

Satiated, exhausted, Nash finally stilled, then slid out of Joshua's body. He smiled and ran a hand down Joshua's back. He pressed a kiss to Joshua's left shoulder. "I think we're going to need a shower and once you've washed me, you can clean up this mess. And boy?"

"Yes, Sir?"

"You can tease me while doing your chores anytime."

Chapter Ten

DR. HOBSON sat across the desk staring at Joshua until Joshua thought he'd burst with the weight of the man's scrutiny. It wasn't only with Nash that Joshua had a love-hate relationship. Dr. Hobson was falling into that category as well. Joshua wasn't even sure why he was there. He should have just canceled. Hell, he should get up right now and run out the goddamn door. Yet, there he sat like some weird virus under a microscope.

Finally, after what seemed an eternity, Dr. Hobson asked, "Why do you feel you don't deserve happiness?"

"I didn't say that," Joshua snapped.

"What exactly did you say, then?" Dr. Hobson countered.

"I said bad things happen when I'm happy."

"Like what?" Dr. Hobson asked in that infuriating calm tone of his.

Joshua gritted his teeth to keep in the *"Fuck you"* that wanted out. Why wasn't he running? He couldn't understand why he wasn't lashing out and getting the hell away from Hobson's scrutinizing gaze and calm fucking questions.

"You seem upset? It was a simple question, Joshua."

"You're damn right I'm upset." Joshua jumped to his feet, but rather than rushing out the door, he started pacing. "I don't know why bad things always happen to me. They just do. It's like every time I get comfortable somewhere, I do something or say something I'm not supposed to, and I fuck everything up." He ran a hand through his hair, fighting the urge to pull it out. "Maybe it's my birthright, born under the wrong sign or some shit. I don't fucking know. You're the doctor. You tell me."

"I can't answer that for you. How about you tell me about the first time you felt content? Happy?"

"No!" Joshua snarled.

"Why not? Is it a secret?" Dr. Hobson inquired.

"No, it's not a big secret. Sheesh. I just don't want to talk about it." Joshua continued to pace, each step heavy, angry.

"What would you like to talk about?"

Joshua stopped midstep and glared at the doctor. "Nothing! I don't want to talk about a goddamn thing! Why do you have to ask me so many questions?"

Dr. Hobson didn't so much as flinch in the face of Joshua's anger. "I'm trying to help you find the answers to yours."

Joshua held Dr. Hobson's gaze a second longer, then stomped away and started pacing again. "Christ, you're irritating me."

"Sounds like everything is irritating you today. Why do you think that is?"

"There you go with your goddamn questions again. Stop it. *Just stop it*!" Joshua curled his hands into fists, digging his fingernails into the meaty flesh of his palms. Blood oozed, the heat flared, and so did the pain, but rather than calm him, it taunted him. His heart hammered, breath harsh. So many damn questions they made his head throb painfully. He continued to stomp around the room, vibrating with a red-hot rage surging through him. Dr. Hobson didn't interfere, only sat at his desk staring at Joshua with that expression that Joshua wanted nothing more than to wipe away with a single blow. He couldn't bear to look at him. Each time he did, it set his blood to boiling, and he'd stomp even harder.

Joshua tried to push away the memories of loss, to focus on the good ones he was making with Nash, but no matter how hard he tried, they'd slip from his mind like smoke, leaving in their place loneliness, hunger, rejection. He started to swipe his arm across the desk, wanted to destroy everything around him, leave it broken as surely as he was. He somehow managed to resist the urge. How long he stayed in that pissed-off state, he wasn't sure. But eventually, it released him, and he slumped down into the chair, exhausted.

"Feel better?" Dr. Hobson inquired.

Joshua rested his elbows on his knees and put his head in his hands. "Not really."

"Would you like something to drink?"

Joshua took a couple of calming breaths, his pulse returning to normal. His temper tantrum left him drained and his throat raw. He lifted his head. "Yes, please," he said hoarsely.

Dr. Hobson picked up the silver decanter, poured ice water into a glass, and handed it to Joshua.

"Thank you." He gulped down a large amount. The cold liquid soothed his painful throat and dry mouth. He finished it, then pushed the empty glass across the desk.

"Would you like some more?"

Joshua lowered his head and closed his eyes. Damn, he was tired. Like bone-deep weary. Not the kind that could be cured with a good night of sleep or even a week's worth. No, this was a weariness born of twenty-five years of struggle.

"I'm not sure it is worth it anymore."

"What's not worth it?"

Joshua snapped his head up and gawked at Dr. Hobson. *Christ, did I say that out loud?* That was a stupid question. He obviously had.

"The struggle." Joshua snapped his mouth shut. His mouth was working faster than his brain.

"Are you having thoughts of hurting yourself?"

All the time. At least this time he was smart enough to keep his big fat stupid mouth shut. "If you're asking me if I'm about to off myself, then the answer is no, so you don't have to worry about calling for the little men in the white coats to put me in a padded room."

Dr. Hobson sat back in his chair, folded his hands, and rested his chin on his thumbs. He stared at Joshua until the weight of it caused Joshua to squirm. "Tell me about this struggle."

"Where should I begin," Joshua said in exasperation.

"From the beginning is always best, I find."

"Dear God, how long do we have? This may take a while."

"I'm in no hurry." Dr. Hobson lowered his hands to his lap and smiled. "I have all afternoon."

"Yeah, well, I don't know if I can handle it that long," Joshua mumbled. He rolled his neck, the tension causing it to crack and pop. "I don't really like thinking about that shit. My past is my past. It needs to stay there."

"Ah, but it's not staying there, is it?"

"Nope. Any suggestion on how to put it back where it belongs, lock it up, and throw away the key?"

"Joshua, we can only hide from our past for so long. It has a way of surfacing, no matter what we do. The best thing is to look at it, learn from it, and move on."

"Oh really? You make it sound so fucking easy," Joshua snapped. It was getting harder and harder to control his temper. To be the perfect little submissive. Hell, right now he didn't want to be. He wanted to kick and scream and fight and destroy anything and everything that reminded him of a time, a day, a moment when he felt weak and helpless. Letting his anger fill him, he glared at Dr. Hobson. "Tell me this. Have you ever watched your mother take the last dime she had to stick a needle in her arm while you were so damn hungry it felt like your stomach was eating itself? Have you ever had to lie on a cold floor and listen to yet another stranger fuck your mother? Have you ever been rescued from one shit hole only to be thrown into another?" With each question his voice rose until he was screaming. He stood, hands flat on the desk, scowling down at Dr. Hobson. "Or worse yet, snatched from a good place and sent to live with a sadistic prick who beat you just for fucking breathing? How many homes were you in by the time you were old enough to run? I bet you didn't sell your ass in a dirty alley just for a meal or a warm place to sleep? So, who in the hell are you to tell me to look at it and move on? Move on from what? Where the fuck am I supposed to move to?"

"This isn't about me, Joshua. This is about you, and as horrible as it sounds, you must do this. Holding all that anger inside is eating you alive."

"You're not fucking listening! *I don't want to*!"

"You've already begun."

Once again, Joshua found himself glaring at the doctor. His heart hammered, beating so hard the rush of blood in his ears was nearly painful in its intensity. *Run. Run. Run!* The voice in his head was getting louder and louder until he thought his eardrums would explode. Only the voice came from within, and he wanted desperately to obey the demand, but he couldn't seem to move. Adrenaline surged through him, his fight-or-flight response fully engaged. He was breathing harshly, body trembling as the battle within raged.

Joshua desperately tried to shove the old memories back into the box, but they refused to be silenced. Instead, it was as if they were swelling, shoving against Joshua's insides, clawing and scratching. He fought back, but it was in vain. He was powerless against his demons. He fell back into the chair, and the tears and memories flowed from him.

SITTING IN his car, Nash checked his watch then the door to Cedric's office for what seemed like the hundredth time. Joshua's appointment should have ended a half hour ago. With each tick of the clock, Nash's unease grew. Had something gone wrong? Was it possible Joshua had gone out the back door? He often wanted to be left alone after a session. However, he'd escape to his bedroom. Joshua had never run from his appointment. Where would he go? They were miles from Nash's home. Nash's unease began to turn to panic, and he reached for the door handle. At that exact moment, Joshua stepped out and stood on the sidewalk, staring up at the bright blue sky.

Nash should have been relieved. However, the look on Joshua's face, his red-rimmed eyes and disheveled appearance caused alarm bells to go off in Nash's mind. After long moments when Joshua continued to stare upward, Nash opened the door and stepped out of the car.

He cautiously approached his boy. "Joshua," he said, keeping his voice low and even. "Are you okay?"

Joshua lowered his gaze, but Nash wasn't sure if Joshua was seeing him. Nash slid his arm around Joshua and gently rubbed his back. "Are you okay?"

Rather than respond, Joshua hugged Nash, hid is face in Nash's neck. Nash wrapped his arms around him, held him as his boy shook so hard Nash feared Joshua would fall.

"I got you," Nash said soothingly. Joshua clung to him as he sobbed. Nash's heart ached for his boy. He wished there was a way he could take all that sadness into himself, so Joshua didn't have to deal with it. But there was no magical or logical thing that could wipe away such anguish. All Nash could do was give him his strength, support Joshua, and be whatever Joshua needed him to be.

Nash held Joshua tighter, stroking his hair until the sobbing quieted into a gentle crying. "Are you ready to go home?"

Joshua nodded.

Nash helped him into the car and buckled him in. Joshua went limp, head hung low. Nash's chest tightened even further to see his boy look so defeated. He needed to get Joshua home, make him feel safe, stabilize him. He patted Joshua's shoulder, then shut the door. He ran around to the driver's side and got behind the wheel. He continued to glance at Joshua as he fired up the car and got them on the road, afraid Joshua would sink further into himself until he disappeared. Nash laid his hand on Joshua's thigh, caressing it, not just to soothe, but because Nash needed the contact with his boy. Joshua kept his head down, wringing his hands, but he was no longer crying and the trembling had eased.

Although it was a short ride home, it felt as if it took forever due to the fact Nash was unable to comfort Joshua. He hated feeling so useless. Something major had happened during Joshua's appointment. Nash could only hope that it was something positive. Sure, Joshua was crying now, but sometimes before someone could get better, they had to face their demons, and Lord knew his poor boy had plenty of those. As painful as it was to see Joshua in this condition, Nash just had to hold on to that glimmer of hope. He pulled into the drive and cut the engine. Joshua instantly opened the door and jumped out of the car.

Nash scrambled to catch up. "Joshua, wait."

Joshua kept walking.

Nash raced forward and caught Joshua's arm, stopping him on the porch. "I said wait." There was no way in hell Nash was going to let Joshua flee to his bedroom. Not this time.

"I just want to go lie down."

"Okay, we'll go stretch out on my bed."

"I—"

"I just want to hold you. That's it. We don't have to talk about what happened."

Joshua looked reluctant.

"Do it for me? Please. I know it may be selfish, but I could use a nap and would love to have you next to me."

Joshua looked down at the hold Nash had on his arm. It shredded Nash's heart that Joshua even had to question it. He had to work harder at earning his boy's trust. If he couldn't trust Nash to take care of him when he was knocked down, how could Nash help him heal? After what seemed an eternity, Joshua finally lifted his head, and the sadness shimmering in his eyes stole Nash's breath. Nash clamped down on it. Joshua was the only thing that mattered, and he needed Nash's support and strength. He had to learn to trust Nash.

"I won't force you to lie down with me, but I hope you will. And in time, I also hope you can open up and talk about what's going on in that pretty head of yours, but I won't force you to do that right now either."

"I can take a nap with you, but that's all I can agree to right now." Joshua's voice trembled when he spoke, but there was a determination in him that couldn't be denied.

Nash kissed Joshua's temple. "That's enough." He then kissed Joshua's lips. "For now."

Nash was willing to give Joshua some time to process whatever demon Cedric had helped to let out of its cage, but not too long. They'd been making great strides, Joshua settling nicely, and this was only a temporary setback. One that was no doubt difficult for his boy, but healing was often painful. Nash would be there every step of the way, Joshua's crutch until he could stand solidly on his own.

~*~

I told him. Dr. Hobson. I told him everything. I have no idea why. I tried to shove the sludge of my childhood back down, but it refused. One minute I was working like hell to get it locked back in the vault, and the next minute it was spewing out of me like a fucking geyser. I haven't ever told anyone, and I'm not sure how I feel about it. On the one hand, it pisses me off, and I swear if, and that's a really big if, I go back to see the doc, I will lose my goddamn mind if he looks at me with pity. I don't want nor do I deserve pity. The shit happened. I've moved on. Period. On the other hand, something happened while I was a total crybaby, or rather after I quit sobbing. The sludge that's always clogging up inside me was gone, and I could breathe. Like, really take a deep breath. I'm sure it's a temporary effect from all that sobbing. It wore me out. All those tears were exhausting. Who knew? Last night I slept better than I have in weeks, months, hell, maybe forever. Maybe it was the exhaustion or Nash's warm body against me, holding me. Hell, maybe it was a combination of both.

This morning I woke up in Nash's bed, those strong, warm arms still around me. I should have felt good, basked in it. I mean, I like sleeping in his bed. It's where I want to be. Only this time when my eyes opened, I looked over at Nash, and instead of feeling content and happy, something like panic rushed in and with it came the sludge. Funny thing is it felt like an old friend. How sad is that?

I don't have much time. I have to make breakfast, and I know Nash is going to want to talk. I don't know what to say to him. I don't know if I can share it again. I don't know if I can show him how weak I am again. I don't know where to go from here. I know I can't go back, but I'm not sure if I have the strength to go forward. I'm not sure about anything anymore. I don't know if I ever was.

Chapter Eleven

SITTING WITH his back against the headboard, Nash sipped his coffee as Joshua moved around in the kitchen. The smell of frying bacon wafted into the room. Breakfast wouldn't be long. Nash had been disappointed when he rolled over as he woke to find Joshua no longer at his side, the feeling quickly replaced with relief when he found Joshua kneeling next to the bed and a tray of coffee sitting on the nightstand. As much as he'd have liked to have a little more snuggling time, it was good to see his boy stick to his routine. Nash was sure it brought Joshua at least a bit of comfort. He did better when he had a routine, when he didn't have to think too much. Nash had almost forgotten that. He'd thought that perhaps they would forgo the discipline, the chores, and the strict schedule. That was for him, not Joshua.

Nash had been in love before, but not like this, not with the consuming need to be the end-all, be-all another person needed him to be. It wasn't just that Joshua needed him. He needed Joshua too. They were two halves of a whole. Dominant and submissive. Lovers and friends. It was the former that he must focus on now. It was part of them. Who they were. There would be plenty of time for dealing with Joshua's session with Cedric later because they would be talking about it. But first things first.

Nash finished his coffee and set the mug on the tray. He slid from the bed, stretched, scratched his belly, then headed for the bathroom. He pissed, washed his hands, and brushed his teeth. He considered taking a quick shower before breakfast but another thought, a better one, popped into his mind.

Nash opened the bathroom door and stuck his head out. "Boy!"

Within seconds, Joshua stood at the end of the hall. "Yes, Sir?"

"Is breakfast done?"

"Yes, Sir. I was just about to plate it."

"Can you keep in on warm?" Nash asked, doing his best to hold back his grin.

Joshua tilted his head. "Umm, yeah, I guess I could put it in the oven on warm. Your toast may not be any good."

"We can make more. Get breakfast set, then join me in the bathroom."

"Yes, Sir."

Nash pulled off his briefs and threw them in the hamper. He hung two thick towels on the hooks next to the shower, then turned on the taps, adjusting the flow to warm. Joshua walked into the room, and Nash stepped in the shower.

"Strip," Nash called out. "I need you to wash me."

"Yes, Sir."

Nash stood beneath the flow of the warm water, hands against the cool tile, and hung his head. He moaned his approval as Joshua began lathering up Nash's back, kneading the muscles as he washed him. Joshua worked up each of Nash's arms, his shoulders, then down his back. Nash spread his legs a little wider as Joshua washed Nash's ass, and his moaning increased as his cock hardened. He hadn't planned on taking Joshua before breakfast, but he should have known. Joshua's hands on him always made Nash want.

Joshua scrubbed Nash's thighs, calves, and then both feet. "If you turn around, I can get the front."

Nash turned, and his erect cock was just inches from Joshua's mouth. Nash smiled down at him. "Proceed, boy."

Joshua poured more soap into his hands and worked up Nash's legs. He took an extra amount of time to wash Nash's balls and dick, stroking and caressing them as he lathered them up. Nash fought the urge to thrust. It felt good, but Joshua still had a job to do.

"All right, boy. I think they are clean enough."

"Yes, Sir," Joshua replied, a hint of amusement in his tone—a sound that did Nash's heart a world of good.

With his stomach and chest squeaky clean, Nash bent his knees to allow Joshua to wash his hair. Once it was all lathered up, he stood beneath the water to rinse away the shampoo.

"My turn." Nash picked up the bodywash and poured a generous amount into his palm. "Arms out."

Joshua held his arms out at his sides and widened his stance. Nash took the same amount of time and care washing his boy. Only when every inch of him had been washed and rinsed did Nash step up, slide his hand around Joshua's waist, pull him close, and take his mouth in a deep and passionate kiss.

Nash eventually ended the kiss, nibbling on Joshua's bottom lip. "You were up and out of bed this morning before I got to do this," Nash whispered against Joshua's lips.

"I'm so—"

"Don't apologize. Just make it up to me."

Joshua grabbed Nash's face in both hands and kissed him until Nash's toes curled and his cock twitched.

"Now that's what I'm talking about," Nash praised when the kiss ended.

"What else can I do to make it up to you, Sir?"

"Well, now that you mention it, I think you may have missed a spot," Nash said slyly. He grabbed Joshua's hand and pressed it against Nash's erection.

"I thought…." Joshua wrapped his fist around Nash's cock and stroked it. "Never mind."

"Good boy." Nash positioned himself in a way that blocked the water from falling down the front side of him. He grabbed the bodywash and squeezed some onto his dick and Joshua's hand. Nash shuddered when the cool liquid hit his heated cockhead. "Hands behind your back."

Joshua did so instantly, and Nash grabbed Joshua's hips in both his hands. He held his boy still while he rutted against him, sliding their equally hard cocks together, the soap slicking the way.

"Look at me," Nash said. Joshua lifted his eyes and held Nash's gaze. "That's it. I want to see those eyes, see the pleasure."

Joshua looked hesitant. Nash was aware that it made his boy uncomfortable, but the look quickly morphed into something else, desire and want, as Nash kept thrusting and rolling his hips. He slid his hands around Joshua's body to grab his ass, blunt fingers digging in, increasing the pressure and friction on their dicks. "Damn, you feel good. So hard against me. Makes me want to bend you over and fuck you through the goddamn wall."

"Do it," Joshua moaned. "Want you."

Nash considered it. He loved Joshua's ass, how tight it was, the way it clamped down on Nash's dick when Joshua came. Unfortunately, the water was already beginning to cool, and ice-cold water beating down his back was counterconducive to what he was chasing. Besides, he didn't have a condom or lube in the shower, and he wasn't about to let go of Joshua long enough to go get them. Hell, he was already close, too close. Nash thrust harder, faster, pulling a deep rumbling moan from his boy.

"That's it. Want to feel you come. Feel you shoot all over my dick…." Nash gritted his teeth. So fucking close. But not yet. "Now, boy. Fucking come on me. Now!"

Joshua's eyes glazed over, face slack, and just as Nash had demanded, he came. Liquid heat fountained over Nash's stomach and dick. It was the last push Nash needed. He dug his fingers in harder to Joshua's ass, back arching, and shot his release against his boy. Perfect timing too, because just then the water turned cold.

"Holy shit," Nash yelped. He released Joshua and spun to shut the tap off.

Joshua snorted.

Nash turned deliberately and narrowed his eyes. "You find something funny, boy?"

Joshua bit his bottom lip and shook his head. He couldn't hide the amusement shining in his eyes nor the way his lip was trembling from obviously trying to hold back his laughter.

"No…. No, Sir." Joshua's words ended on a snort.

"Uh-huh." Nash grabbed a towel and tossed it at Joshua. Nash looked down his body and shook his head. "So much for cleaning me up. Look at this mess you made." He took the other towel and ran it down his chest. He tensed when the terrycloth swiped over his overly sensitive dick.

"Sorry, Sir. I can make that up to you as well."

"Oh, you'll make it up to me all right," Nash assured him. He pressed a quick kiss to Joshua's mouth. "But first, morning discipline and breakfast."

AN ORGASM was a great way to start any day, but Joshua was still waiting for the other shoe to drop. Nash had been heavy-handed with his morning discipline, which Joshua was extremely thankful for. It gave him an opportunity to concentrate on his ass during breakfast rather than what had happened the day before, what Nash would no doubt want to talk about. Joshua still hadn't decided if he would or could go there. Fortunately for him, he wouldn't have to decide right away. Nash was holed up in his office on some conference call, and Joshua had chores to do.

He sprayed down the tile in the shower stall with disinfectant and smiled to himself as he started scrubbing. Thinking about what had happened in this very space just a few hours ago was a lot more pleasurable to think about than….

Nope, he wasn't going there. Only the harder he tried to think about Nash rubbing off on him, the more those damn memories from the day before kept sneaking in and ruining his happiness. Wasn't that always the way it went? The bad always seemed to upstage the good. At least that was the way it was in Joshua's world. He hadn't been lying when he told Dr. Hobson that. He hadn't been complaining, but simply stating a fact. He'd grown used to it. At least he thought he had. The session yesterday, the tears, the comfort Nash showed him, everything that had happened from the moment he'd walked into the doc's office to this second, the only thing he was acutely aware of was his confusion. That, like the sludge, was an old friend and as odd as it seemed, hell, he welcomed it. Certainly was easier to deal with than crying over shit he couldn't change.

He finished wiping down the walls and turned on the tap to rinse it. He then moved on to the other fixtures in the bathroom, setting aside the bullshit thoughts and running a mental list in his head of what he needed to accomplish today. There were floors to be scrubbed, laundry to be done, and dinner to think of. Those things he could control.

"Joshua?" Nash called out.

"I'm in the hall bathroom."

Seconds later, Nash's smiling face became visible from the door. "You got plans tonight?"

Joshua started to roll his eyes but caught himself at the last second. "Only the ones you make for me, Sir."

"Great! You're having dinner with Denny."

"What?"

"Malcolm called. He wants to talk to me about some plans he has for expanding the club. He thought it would be a good opportunity for our boys to get out. I agree with him."

"What about you? Should I prepare your meal before I go?"

"Nah, I'll get something at the club. You're off duty tonight. Go have fun."

Joshua tensed. He liked Denny, enjoyed his company the time they'd had lunch together, but Joshua wasn't sure if he could go there tonight. There was nothing to keep his mind occupied and keep the shit from pouring out of him again. He wasn't ready. He couldn't. He began to tremble. Not a good idea. He couldn't—

"Hey, hey," Nash said soothingly and ran his fingers through Joshua's hair. "It's just dinner with a friend. No pressure. You don't have to. I just thought it would be good for you to enjoy some time with Denny, laugh, have fun, and just be for one night."

The tension in Joshua began to ease beneath Nash's gentle touch and calm voice. Nash was right. Why he was panicking? He wasn't sure. Maybe this was the perfect opportunity to put the previous day behind him. Would definitely go further to keep him occupied than scrubbing floors and ironing.

He took a deep breath and looked up to meet Nash's concerned gaze. "I'm sorry. Not sure where that came from. Of course I'd like to hang out with Denny."

Nash held out his hand and Joshua took it, allowing Nash to help him to his feet. "Wise choice, boy. And if you aren't having fun or it becomes too much, you call me and I'll be right there to bring you home, okay?"

"Yes, Sir. Thank you."

"You're welcome." Nash kissed his forehead. "But I'm sure you'll be fine. In fact, I know you will."

Glad someone is. Joshua, on the other hand, wasn't as convinced, but he was willing to try anything to get the thoughts out of his head. Even if only for a little while.

Chapter Twelve

NOT TRUSTING himself to be out in public with his nerves still so raw, Joshua had suggested Nash let him cook for Denny. Thankfully, Nash had agreed. Dinner was chicken alfredo, basically, a meal in a box; not Joshua's favorite but it was one of Denny's favorites. The only thing that would be lacking from a crappy Italian dinner was a cheap bottle of red wine. Which was probably just as well, considering Denny's flighty disposition and that it made Joshua's brooding personality even darker. Although Joshua liked Denny, he really wasn't in the mood for company, and he'd rather eat anything other than alfredo. Still, when the doorbell rang, Joshua hurried to answer it.

Denny grinned and jumped at Joshua as soon as he'd opened the door. He threw his arms around Joshua, hugging him tightly. "Hey, sexy man, how are you? Wow! It smells great in here," Denny rambled, all smiles.

Denny was adorable and had a way of pulling Joshua out of his crappy mood with one smile, and Joshua couldn't help but return it. The feel-good vibes were temporary, but for now, it was fun, and Joshua went with it.

"It's amazing what you can do with some noodles and a jar of sauce. Come on in."

"Whatever. You can't get such yummy scents out of a jar." Denny followed Joshua, sticking close. "I'm starving. Feed me, sweet man."

Joshua laughed, pointed to a barstool at the counter where he'd set out plates and silverware, then went to the stove. "You don't get a lot of home cooking, do you?"

"Kind of hard when you live at a club," Denny said absently. Joshua looked over to see him riffling through the newspaper Nash had left on the counter during lunch. "Don't get me wrong, the restaurant there has some amazing food and the chefs highly talented. It's just I don't like for them to have to go out of their way for me. Besides, I can't really afford those dinner prices." Denny chuckled.

"Now I feel bad I didn't put more effort into our dinner." Joshua put a pile of pasta in the center of Denny's plate and then some on his own. "What can I get you to drink?"

Denny swirled his fork into his fettuccini and shoved a large amount into his mouth. He chewed happily with a big grin on his face. "Oh. My. God. This is even better than it smells." He gathered up another large number of noodles and brought the fork to his mouth. "Water is fine," he said before taking another big bite.

Joshua grabbed two glasses of ice water, sat one down in front of Denny, then put the other next to his own plate before sitting across from Denny. "Okay, you got me. It's homemade, but if I'd known you only ever eat at the club, I would have put more time and effort into it."

"If it's got cream, noodles, and chicken, and not being served out of a restaurant kitchen, then in my book, it's the perfect home-cooked meal." Denny grinned again and dug into his plate with gusto.

Joshua pushed his food around with his fork. It did smell good. What the hell. He took a small bite. It was actually better than he'd expected. He took another bite, chewing slowly and giving Denny time to enjoy his meal before speaking again.

"So how are things going with you and Malcolm?"

Denny took the last bite on his plate, literally vibrating while he wiped his mouth on a napkin. He then grinned hugely and jumped to his feet. "Look." He turned his back to Joshua, pulled off his sweatshirt, and tugged his T-shirt up to his shoulders. "Malcolm took me on stage last night."

Denny's back was a crosshatch pattern of red marks from shoulder to the lumbar area. Joshua pushed to his feet and moved around the counter without taking his eyes off Denny's back. He traced the marks with the tip of his finger, feeling the warmth of Denny's reddened skin. Joshua hadn't been put through that kind of a workout in a very long time. Jealousy bubbled up inside him and he choked it down.

"Damn, Denny, this is beautiful."

"Master Malcolm has a very good hand. I don't remember all of it. I mean, I remember the pain. Holy fuck, do I ever. I wasn't sure I was going to be able to handle it, and I tell ya, I thought I was going to pass out or piss myself or lose my fucking mind. Which, come to think of it, I think I did lose my mind, because the rest of it is a little hazy." Denny chuckled. He was making light of it, but there was pride in his tone, and it made Joshua all the more envious. "Master Malcolm says that I pleased him very much and that when he finally let me get off, I was begging. Honestly? All I remember is coming to in the back room with Master Malcolm tending my back."

"And what a work of art it is," Joshua whispered, still tracing the marks gently. This was what he needed. To be put through something this intense until he was flying high, far, far, away from his own mind. The jealousy left a bitter taste in his mouth. He cleared his throat and stepped back. "Did you get punished for losing it at the end?" he asked, going back around the counter and picking up the plates. He turned and put the dirty dishes in the sink, unable to meet Denny's gaze, not wanting his own issues to damper Denny's excitement.

"In the process." Denny shrugged his jacket back on, then grabbed his crotch. "I have a feeling I won't be getting rid of this fucking cage anytime soon. But totally worth it." He smiled, a dreamy expression on his face as he no doubt was remembering what had transpired to be given such a punishment.

"I can tell from the glint in your eye, it really was worth it," Joshua said.

"Oh yeah," Denny said with a grin and a nod. "Anyway, how are things going with you and Nash? I haven't seen you guys at the club, and Malcolm simply refuses to gossip." He wore a pouty expression.

"Things are okay." Joshua brought the dishrag to the counter. "Nash has been keeping me busy."

"You'll have to be more specific with the *busy*." Denny waved his arm dramatically and knocked over his water. "Oh damn, my bad." He plucked the dishcloth from Joshua's hand and sopped up the water. "I can be such a frickin' klutz."

"It's okay, Denny. It's just water." Joshua rushed to the sink and grabbed a dry towel. He knelt on the floor and wiped up the water that had run down the island and onto the tile.

Denny bounded around to the other side of the island, hands on his lean hips while he smiled down at Joshua. "I can see why your Dom likes to see you on your knees. You're so damn sexy when you kneel."

"Denny," Joshua said warningly as he finished cleaning up the spill. Joshua knew Denny didn't mean anything by his teasing. The little shit was a constant tease, but Joshua wasn't going to encourage his impish behavior. As he got back to his feet, he looked at Denny. "What would Master Malcolm say if he heard you trying to hit on me?" He moved to the sink and tossed the towel in it.

"You aren't going to snitch on me, are you?" Denny asked. Joshua looked back to see the cocky grin on Denny's handsome face.

"I promise not to if you'll behave." Denny pushed out his bottom lip and batted his long lashes. He looked like a cute puppy. He could see why Malcolm was drawn to him. He really was quite irresistible. "Not going to work on me. Now sit your ass down, and I may just share the dessert I made."

"Oh, what did you make?"

"You'll have to promise before I tell you." Joshua arched a brow in challenge.

Denny studied Joshua carefully for a moment. It appeared he was trying to decide if fucking with Joshua was worth giving up dessert. "You are a cruel, cruel hotty man." He sighed dramatically. "Fine, sweets, bring me some treats. Ooh, I just sounded like a poet." Denny giggled.

Joshua rolled his eyes, then went to the refrigerator and retrieved the strawberry cheesecake he'd made. Hopefully Denny liked it. If not, he'd made chocolate chip cookies too, because, yeah, everyone liked those. He set the dessert on the island, and Denny's eyes lit up.

"Oh. My. God. Did you make that?"

"From scratch," Joshua said with a little pride.

"Marry me."

Denny reached out and stuck his finger in the cheesecake. Joshua slapped his hand. "So much for behaving," he chastised.

"I can't help it. I gave that promise before I knew you made not only my favorite dinner but my favorite dessert too. You know what they say is the best way to a man's heart."

Joshua pulled a knife from the block, drew it through the cake, and grinned. "A riding crop and a heavy hand?"

"Oh, I do like the way you think." Denny snickered and winked at Joshua. "I was talking about through their stomachs, but I like your idea."

"Fewer calories too," Joshua said and set a large slice of dessert in front of Denny.

"Bitch, are you saying I'm fat?"

Joshua held up his hands in defense. "I would never. You've got the cutest, perkiest ass I've ever seen."

Denny pushed out his chest and danced a little. "I really do," he said in agreement.

"Pure perfection."

"That's the honest truth." Denny puckered up and blew Joshua a kiss. He picked up his fork, cut the tip off the cake, and popped it into his mouth. "Mmm, this is so good I could come."

"Don't you dare," Joshua chastised. "Malcolm will never believe you had a foodgasm."

"Sad but true, and my poor back and cock can't handle anything more today. But it really is very good. Well done."

Denny was such a sweet guy with a bubbly personality. It was like happiness oozed from him. Joshua envied him that. He was glad he agreed to have dinner with Denny, but still, he couldn't let that little nagging voice go, the one that said he might end up embarrassing himself in front of Denny. His nerves were a bit raw. He'd taken a hell of a hit to any confidence he might have pretended to have. All he could do was try to keep his shit together and not let the conversation drift toward anything too deep.

"Thanks, I'm glad you like it," Joshua finally said. He took a bite of the cheesecake. He had to admit, it was good.

"I mean it. This is super delish." Denny took another big bite. "How long do you think the Doms will be doing their Dommy stuff?"

"I don't know. Nash didn't say how long he'd be. Why? Did you have plans?"

"No, I was just thinking cuddling up on the couch and watching a good movie would be the cherry on top of this delightful dinner party for two."

"That sounds awesome." It really did, and Joshua would love the distraction. "What kind of movies do you like?"

Denny halted his fork almost to his mouth and pursed his lips. "Hmm, well, I like horror, but trust me, you do not want to watch one with me. I have a very high-pitched scream, and honey, I will use it." He took the last bite of his cheesecake, set the fork down, then wiped his mouth with his napkin before continuing. "I love action-adventure and sci-fi. You're safe if you watch one of those with me."

"Seriously?" Joshua asked as he studied Denny. "I don't know why, but I would have guessed maybe musicals or chick flicks would have been your favorites."

"Oh no, you didn't." Denny narrowed his eyes. "I think you may have just insulted my manlihood."

"Manlihood?" Joshua laughed, then patted Denny's arm. "I would never insult a man's manlihood, especially yours. I only meant that you're always so bubbly, happy, that I would think you liked more upbeat, positive-type shows, instead of death and mayhem or, God forbid, little alien creatures ripping their way out of a guy's stomach."

"I totally loved *Alien*, and that scene was pure badassery. I mean seriously, think of the limits in computers and special effects in 1979, and they nailed the realism!" Denny pushed his empty plate away and pointed to it. "Please take that away before I beg you for another piece, and trust me, I'm really, really good at begging."

"I'm sure you are." Joshua chuckled. "You're more than welcome to have more. I made plenty."

Denny shook his head. "Thanks, but no thanks. I'm watching my figure, and I know you are too. You don't fool me. I saw you check out my ass."

"Of course I did. You have a sweet ass." Joshua stood up, smiling. "Let me throw these plates in the dishwasher, and we'll go see what's on TV." He took their plates to the sink and turned on the faucet.

"Need some help?" Denny offered.

"I got these, but if you want to put the dessert in the fridge, I'd appreciate it."

"Anything for you, hotty man."

Joshua shook his head, smiling as he quickly loaded the dishwasher. He dried his hands, dropped the towel on the counter, then grabbed Denny's hand. "C'mon." Joshua plopped down on the couch, tugging Denny down with him. Joshua picked up the remote and handed it to Denny. "Pick whatever you want."

"Cool. I like hanging with you. Malcolm never lets me pick the show. Don't tell him but if I have to watch one more rerun of *The Golden Girls*, I swear he's going to be the one getting spanked."

"I'd seriously like to see that."

"Me too." Denny giggled. He shifted, snuggling into Joshua's side, legs stretched out on the couch. He clicked on the TV and started going through the channels.

Worried Denny might try to ask him questions while he channel-surfed, Joshua decided to be the one to keep the focus on something other than him. "So are things getting serious between you and Malcolm? Have you two talked contract?"

The way Denny tensed was impossible to miss. "No, he hasn't even mentioned it. I mean, I take care of him, and he takes care of me. He…. Well… it's okay the way things are."

"From the way you tensed and the tone of your voice, it doesn't sound like you're okay with it."

Denny shrugged and shifted a bit. "I don't know. I guess in some aspects it works and in other ways not so much. I serve him, I do what I'm told, and he gives me the structure I need. I'm learning a lot about my submission, and it's rewarding at times. And, honey, don't get me started on how mind-blowingly good the sex is between us. Like off-the-fucking-charts hot. I should be happy, content but… I don't know. It feels like it's more for fun when it should be meaningful."

Joshua could imagine how hard that was. Not belonging. Hell, who was he kidding? He didn't have to imagine. He knew exactly how it felt. He'd been an outcast all his life. Even with Nash. Sure, he had a contract, so in a sense, he belonged to Nash, just as he'd belonged to Troy and…. He shook his head. *Not going there*.

"Maybe you should talk to Malcolm? Tell him what you need."

Denny shrugged again. "I don't think that's a good idea. I have to trust that he knows what I need. Just like you trust Nash."

It was Joshua's turn to tense, but he recovered quickly, forcing himself to go limp. "Are you just going to play with the remote all night, or are you actually going to pick something?" He didn't want to talk anymore because, with the sadness in Denny's tone, he surely would want to do the same as Joshua had been doing, redirect the topic of conversation. That's wasn't a place Joshua wanted to go.

"Oh look!" Denny squealed. "*Tron*!"

"Never seen it."

Denny looked up at him in obvious shock. "You're shitting me, right?"

"Nope."

"Dude, it's hard to understate how much this film changed the genre of science fiction. It's the first movie to use computer-generated effects. You'll love it."

"I'm sure I will." Even if he didn't, it would still be better than talking about feels. In fact, he loved the movie already.

Chapter Thirteen

NASH PACED the small confines of Malcolm's office like a caged animal. He shouldn't have let Malcolm talk him into this. Joshua needed him, not a dinner date with Denny. What had he been thinking? Dammit, apparently he hadn't been thinking, or he wouldn't be here. He'd be home with his boy.

"I don't mean to disrupt your toddler tantrum, but would you mind not wearing a path in my rug?"

Nash stopped his stomping and glared at Malcolm. "You have no idea what I'm going through."

"I have an idea, but that is no reason to take it out on my poor rug." Malcolm sniffed.

Nash slumped down in the chair across the desk from Malcolm. "What do you think they are talking about?"

"I have no idea, but whatever the topic of conversation, I am sure your boy is fine. Denny has a way of easing people. He's such a kind soul with a flighty attitude, which makes him impossible not to love."

"Yeah, if it's so impossible, when are you going to make him your boy?" Nash countered.

Malcolm sighed dramatically. "He is sweet and fun but much too young for me. I'm simply taking him under my wing until he is ready and able to commit to a master."

Nash didn't miss the sadness in Malcolm's tone as he spoke of a master for Denny. The longing and fondness for the boy was evident. "I thought you always said age is just a number?"

"It is, but a boy thirteen years my junior makes me feel old."

"Yet, you realize the boy is a twenty-seven-year-old man who is head over heels for you," Nash pointed out. "Besides, I know you care deeply for him. Why let a number come between your happiness, and his?"

Malcolm waved a dismissive hand. "I thought you were here to help me with the expansion plans, not talk about my love life."

"So you admit you love him," Nash countered.

"I said no such thing."

"You didn't have to."

Malcolm pushed the blueprints across the desk toward Nash. "What do you think of the location of the locker room?"

Nash glanced at the prints, then back to Malcolm. "Nice deflection, but it won't work. You've been smitten with Denny since the first time you laid eyes on him."

"As you were with Joshua."

"Exactly! So I really don't understand your hesitation."

"He's much—"

Nash frowned. "Don't you dare. He's a grown man, so the age difference argument isn't going to work."

"You are quite the pain in the derriere."

"I can be," Nash said slyly.

Malcolm stared at Nash briefly with an exasperated expression on his face. Finally, he sighed again. "I'll consider your argument if you will help me with these damn expansion plans."

Nash laughed. He knew Malcolm well enough that there would be no more talk on the subject of Denny. However, he also knew Malcolm would, in fact, be considering what Nash had said. He hadn't been lying. The age difference was a silly argument, one that should have no bearing on two people who were obviously in love. Nash moved his chair closer to the desk and turned the blueprints around to study them. He didn't miss the cocky grin on Malcolm's face. He obviously thought he'd won. Silly man.

Nash scanned the plans, which included a gym, locker room, as well as public and private baths. The club, including the restaurant, was financially successful, and Nash had no doubt the proposed additions would only add to that success.

Malcolm went on and on about mosaic tile, fixtures, lighting, and gym equipment. He spent an extended amount of time on hot bodies, sweat, and flexed muscles, and it took Nash a while to get the man back on track. Still, it kept Nash's mind and focus on the here and now, instead of what was happening back home.

Home.

Joshua.

Nash glanced at the clock—ten after eight—and jumped up. "Holy shit! I gotta go. I told Joshua I'd be home at eight."

Malcolm leaned back in his chair and stretched his arms over his head. "Time does fly when you're having fun."

Nash slid his shoes on and grabbed his coat. He hated to be late. Joshua would probably be worried sick.

Malcolm picked up the phone and dialed. "Have Mel bring the car around for Master Nash, please." He hung up the phone and went to his feet. He moved around his desk to stand next to Nash. "Thank you for all your help."

"You're welcome."

Malcolm slung his arm around Nash's shoulder. "C'mon, my friend, I'll walk you out."

AN UNEASY feeling settled over Nash, his heart beating rapidly as he hurried up the walkway toward the dark house. He tried the front door and found it locked. His pulse kicked up another notch. His hands were shaking when he pulled his keys from his pocket and unlocked the door. The house was silent.

"Joshua!" Nash called out. He rushed into the house, a flickering light coming from the living room.

Nash let out a pent-up breath when he found Joshua and Denny snuggled up on the couch in front of the TV. Joshua lifted his head and rubbed his eyes. "Oh, hi, Sir. Sorry, I must have dozed off. What time is it?"

"Eight thirty."

Joshua smiled sleepily. He glanced over at Denny, then nudged him gently. "Denny, time to get up."

"I don't want to," Denny grumbled. He rolled, threw his arm over Joshua, and buried his face in Joshua's chest.

"Boy! Your car is waiting."

Denny jerked upright so quickly he nearly fell off the couch. Only Joshua's quick reflexes saved the boy from landing on his ass. "S-sorry, Sir. I didn't hear you come in."

"That's quite all right." Nash walked over to the couch and ruffled Denny's hair. "Mel is waiting to take you home."

"Thanks for the dinner and movie." Denny pecked Joshua on the cheek, then stood up. He turned to Nash. "Thank you for allowing me to come over and hang out with Joshua, Sir. He's a wicked good cook and even better snuggler."

"You're welcome, and yes I am aware."

"Night, Joshua. Night, Master Nash," Denny called out as he rushed to the door.

Nash waited until he heard the door open and close before he sat on the couch next to Joshua. "How was your dinner?"

"Surprisingly good. Denny really seemed to like it."

"Of course he did. You're a great cook." Nash nodded to the TV. "Sounds like dinner was more successful than the movie. You were both out cold when I came in."

"Yes, Sir. Denny likes sci-fi, at least he claims to. He fell asleep before I did. I really wasn't into it but couldn't reach the remote without disturbing him, so…." Joshua shrugged, then yawned.

Nash grabbed the remote and clicked the TV off. "I'm in need of a hot shower before bed, and I'm in need of someone to scrub my back."

"Mmm, I volunteer, Sir."

The happiness in Joshua's tone did Nash's heart good. Malcolm had been right, as usual. Joshua needed time to decompress after his intense meeting with Cedric. Still, Nash was curious what had been discussed during the session. In time, his boy would open up and discuss it with Nash—when he was ready. Hopefully that would be sooner rather than later, or Nash just might seriously go crazy.

Nash patted Joshua's thigh. "All right, boy, go get the shower started."

"Yes, Sir." Joshua scrambled from the couch and hurried to the bathroom.

Joshua's tight little butt swayed with each step. Inspiration hit Nash, and he stopped by his bedroom to retrieve some lube and a plug. A wet, naked Joshua was hard to resist, but a wet, naked, happy Joshua—impossible. In the bathroom, he found Joshua standing next to the shower stall with a sly grin. The enclosure glass was already beginning to steam up.

"Strip," Nash ordered. While Joshua removed his clothes, Nash briefly set his items down to shrug out of his own clothes, then grabbed Joshua's hand and pulled him into the shower. He didn't miss the way Joshua's gaze kept settling on the plug or his obvious arousal at the sight.

"Lean forward, hands on the wall, and push that ass out."

"My pleasure, Sir." Joshua instantly got into position.

Nash squeezed a small amount of lube onto the plug and swiped his fingers over it until it was covered. He pressed one slick finger against Joshua's hole, then tapped and teased it before pushing just the tip of his finger in to the first joint. He rotated his finger gently, knowing it wasn't nearly enough for his boy, but Nash wanted to go slow, enjoying his growing arousal. Joshua pushed his ass out, begging with his body. Nash laid his hand on Joshua's right buttcheek and dug his blunt fingers into the meaty flesh, steadying his movements. This was his show, and he refused to be rushed.

Joshua stilled, but his body was tense. The anticipation grew in the small space, mixing and mingling with the rising steam until it arced in charged electricity. Only then did Nash push his finger deeper into Joshua. Nash curled his finger and hit Joshua's sweet spot, pulling a deep rumbling moan from Joshua. Nash pegged it a few more times, then withdrew his finger.

"Sir, please," Joshua whimpered.

Nash didn't torture his boy. He pressed the tip of the lubed plug against Joshua's hole, putting slight pressure on it, transfixed as Joshua's body slowly opened to him. When the widest part of the plug had breached Joshua, Nash halted. Joshua's ass contracted around the toy, trying to adjust to the invasion. Finally, Nash pushed it deep and settled the wide base flush against Joshua's asscheeks. Nash jiggled it a couple of times, then slapped Joshua's right buttcheek, causing him to jerk.

"All right, boy, wash me before the water turns cold."

"Yes, Sir," Joshua responded, voice tight. He turned gingerly. It was obvious he was worried about the lubed plug sliding out as it wasn't only his voice that was tight but his muscles as well. More proof of the struggle was Joshua's clenched jaw.

Nash caught sight of Joshua's straining prick, and it was too much of a temptation. While Joshua soaped up his hands and lathered Nash's chest, Nash swiped his hand through the soap, then wrapped it around Joshua's cock, stroking him as he washed Nash's chest and stomach. Nash's ministrations made it difficult for Joshua to wash all of Nash, but Nash wasn't worried so much about cleanliness at the moment. He refused to release his hold on Joshua's dick. He liked the feel of it against his palm and the little porn noises Joshua was making.

"You're going to have to turn around if you want me to wash your back, Sir."

"Hold out your hands," Nash ordered. When Joshua complied, Nash grabbed the bodywash and poured a good amount into Joshua's palm. He then set the bottle down, grabbed Joshua, and pulled him close. They both hissed when their hard cocks came into contact. "Now you can reach my back. Problem solved."

"That it is, Sir." Joshua laughed.

Nash took his mouth in a blistering kiss, pulling Joshua's happiness into him, causing sparks against his tongue and a tingling sensation to race across his flesh. He slid his lips over Joshua's cheek to his ear, then scraped his teeth over the sensitive flesh beneath it.

"Don't forget my ass," he teased.

"I'd never forget such a fine, fine specimen, Sir."

Nash nipped Joshua's skin again. "Good answer, boy." He lapped at the water droplets running down Joshua's neck, then sucked up a mark while Joshua ran his soapy hands along Nash's body. They were both moving, hands roaming and stroking. They barely got clean before the water began to cool. It was the only thing that penetrated Nash's lust, and he released his hold on Joshua and turned off the tap, then grabbed a couple of towels and handed one to Joshua.

Joshua quickly tied it around his waist and took the other one from Nash. "Here, let me, Sir."

While Joshua dried Nash, Nash couldn't help but think how funny it was that such a simple act caused his chest to swell with pride. It was sweet and selfless, evidence his boy wasn't at the moment trying to manipulate him but truly wanted to please him without the promise of reward. Considering Joshua was working with a rock-hard cock and a plug in his ass, that he could focus on Nash at all was huge. Nash wanted to kiss him or fuck him or both. Now.

"On my bed, boy. Hands and knees."

"Yes, Sir."

Nash ripped the towel from around Joshua's waist, then took the other from his hands and dropped them both on the floor. Nash followed his boy and had to bite down on his bottom lip to keep from laughing. Joshua's normal gracefully gait was jerky and tight to maintain a hold on the plug while he walked. It was too damn cute.

Standing next to the bed, Joshua tilted his head. "Would you like me to pull the covers back first, Sir?"

"Yes, thank you for thinking about my poor bedspread."

Joshua turned down the covers, then climbed up onto the mattress and got into the position Nash had instructed.

Nash grabbed another lube packet from the bedside table, then joined him. He went to his knees behind his boy. He played with the plug, pulling it out slightly then pushing it deep again. He repeated the movement over and over. Joshua was swaying, muscles flexing. He was literally vibrating. He clamped down on the sheet so hard his knuckles turned white, but he remained silent.

That's about to change, Nash thought wryly.

He opened the condom and rolled it down his length. This time when he grasped the plug, he pulled it slowly from Joshua's body and set it aside. He lined up the head of his cock against Joshua's hole, then pushed in deep in one fluid movement.

"Ah God," Joshua moaned lowly.

Nash smiled and grabbed Joshua's hips in both hands, holding tight. He set up a hard and fast rhythm, fucking his boy with gusto. Within moments Joshua was babbling, groaning, and taking every fucking stroke Nash pounded into him. The loud sound of skin slapping skin echoed around the room, growing in volume, as did the sexy noises coming from Joshua.

"You're not to come," Nash gritted out without slowing down.

"Ye…Y-Yes, Sir," Joshua responded, sounding less than sure of himself.

However, Nash knew his boy would follow his orders. Besides, he wouldn't have to wait long. Joshua's ass felt too fucking good around his cock; each contraction of the tight passage, each thrust pushed Nash closer to the edge. He really should have more control, but dammit, the pleasure was so intense and he didn't want to be denied. Nash eased Joshua down, pinning him with his body. He took Joshua's hands in his and raised them over Joshua's head. They were touching from head to toe, skin to gloriously hot, slick skin. Nash rolled his hips, making short stabbing movements into Joshua's ass.

He brushed his lips over Joshua's ear. "Your ass feels so good. I love fucking you. The way you take it. The…." Nash's voice caught. He stilled and squeezed his eyes shut, trying his best to stave off the inevitable. But it was impossible. He'd waited too long. He snapped his hips, pounding into Joshua as his orgasm rolled down his spine. "Come for me," he gritted out, just as he began to come. Pulse after pulse he filled the condom deep inside his boy, keeping a jerky rhythm until his boy cried out his name.

Nash lay on Joshua for several moments, basking in the postorgasmic glow until his heart and breath returned to normal. Only then did he slide from Joshua's body and dispose of the condom in the trash can next to the bed. He rolled a sleepy and satisfied Joshua out of the wet spot, pulled the top sheet over them, and wrapped his arms around his boy. They had a lot to discuss,

but not tonight. Tonight he was content to soak in Joshua's warmth
and happiness.

~*~

*If I could build a bubble around myself, I would construct it
with impermeable material and a foolproof lock. I'd only allow
good things in my bubble. It would contain a large-screen TV, an
endless supply of great movies—it would include* Doom, *20-ounce
cans of Coke, and hot buttered popcorn filled with peanut M&Ms.
A large comfortable couch, even bigger soft bed, kind of like what
was in Nash's house. In fact, Nash's house would be allowed in.
I like it as it is, except the TV would have to be bigger. Nash and
Denny could come in my bubble, but they would have to check
their pasts at the door. No reality allowed. My little world would be
warm, comfortable, and nothing but good vibes. No bad thoughts,
heartbreak, or judgment. The way I felt hanging out with Denny.
The intensity of sweet lovemaking, the feeling of being loved and
protected in Nash's arms afterward. Those are the feelings that
would shine brightest twenty-four seven.*

*At night I construct my world, decorate it, fill it, everything in
its place. Then, just as I have it ready, I can see Nash and Denny,
smiling, waving me to come inside. I open the door and....*

*I wake up to my reality. I hide my tears of loss. Swallow them
down, pull myself from the bed, go make coffee, and wait for the
dream to come again.*

I'm always waiting.

Chapter Fourteen

HEAD BOWED, Joshua knelt silently next to Nash's bed, waiting for him to wake. Joshua both looked forward to Nash opening his eyes and dreaded it in equal measure. The bubble would burst. It always did. The day before had started out at a major low point and ended on a high note. He was literally shaking with dread of what the day had in store for him. The roller-coaster ride he'd been on since meeting Nash now roiled Joshua's gut, not from the thrill of the ride but from the constant rapid descent from the high peaks.

Not sure how much longer I can take this. Joshua ran his hands over his face, then through his sweat-dampened hair. His nerves were shot. He hated the constant ups and downs. Hated that he couldn't trust in something good. Hated that he wanted those good things more than anything, yet dreaded them. Most of all, he hated that his head was so fucked-up.

"Good morning, boy."

Joshua snapped his head up, met Nash's gaze, then quickly lowered his eyes. "Good morning, Sir." Joshua cringed at the sound of his weak voice. He pushed his morose thoughts down as best as he could. "How did you sleep?" This time his voice was stronger. He picked up the tray on the bedside table, and when Nash sat up to lean against the headboard, Joshua set the tray on his lap.

"I slept like a champ. I always sleep better curled up next to you." Nash picked up his stainless-steel mug, removed the lid, and took a small sip of the steaming brew. "I think we'll make that a permanent rule."

"What's that, Sir?"

"That you have to keep that warm body of yours close to me while I sleep." Nash winked, then took another sip.

"Yes, Sir." Joshua went to his feet, keeping his head low, and avoided looking at Nash. His flight response kicked in, and suddenly he needed to move, to get out of Nash's presence. "Breakfast will be ready shortly. Would you like to eat it here or in the dining room?"

Nash cocked his head. "No comment on my new rule?"

"Whatever pleases you, Sir," he replied robotically. Sleeping in Nash's bed was something Joshua had wanted. Hell, how many times had he lain in his own bed, bitching and fuming for being denied? He didn't understand why it bothered him now that he was getting what he wanted, but it did.

"What would please me is to have my warm and happy sub from last night back." Nash set his coffee down, then placed the tray on the side table. He stretched out and lifted the covers, exposing his naked body. "Come back to bed."

Joshua bit his lip and glanced at the door. "What about breakfast?"

"Is there any concern it will burn the house down?"

Joshua didn't understand his hesitation. Why was he considering lying about breakfast just so he could flee the room? It made no sense. Nash was staring at him expectantly, holding the covers up, and Joshua didn't have time to figure out what he was feeling.

He couldn't push the lie past his lips so he simply said, "No, Sir."

"Is there another reason I'm sitting here getting a chill?"

Joshua started to apologize, but again he had no idea why. God he was a frickin' mess. Without another word, he crawled onto the bed to lie next to Nash.

Nash dropped the sheet over them, then wrapped his arms around Joshua, kissed the top of his head. "Now how about that happy?"

"Sorry, I'm kind of distracted this morning."

"Care to share what's going on in this pretty head of yours?" Nash kissed Joshua's forehead.

Joshua wasn't even sure what he was feeling, so there was no way he could explain it to Nash even if he wanted to. And part of him did, a big part, because somewhere deep inside, he held on to the hope that Nash could fix whatever was broken inside him. He lay there with Nash, holding him. The random patterns Nash was making on Joshua's arm with the tip of his finger were soothing. Yet Joshua tensed further. It was like he was a beat-up tin toy and the key that made him work was being wound tighter and tighter and tighter. Eventually the tension would become too much and he'd either break apart or quietly and simply stop working. He knew Nash was waiting for him to say something, but he couldn't. The key just kept turning.

"Does it have something to do with your session with Dr. Hobson?" Nash prompted.

The key turned again, tighter.

"Why would you think that?" Joshua asked. He instantly regretted saying anything.

Nash slid his palm over Joshua's jaw, urging him to turn his head and look at him. Joshua obeyed but was unable to meet Nash's gaze. It didn't matter that Joshua wanted to avoid the conversation because Nash kept talking.

"You had a good time with Denny, and you and I had a great night. It's the only thing I can think of that would put you in such a morose mood."

Joshua unconsciously pushed into the warm touch even as he mentally kicked himself for not hiding his emotions better. He didn't want to talk about what happened with Dr. Hobson again— the first time had been hard enough.

"You witnessed the aftermath. You can't possibly want to see me blubbering and sobbing again," Joshua muttered.

"I don't like seeing you cry, but I'd rather you share your tears with me than keep it all bottled up inside." Nash tapped gently on Joshua's chest over his heart. "In there it festers and grows until it will eat you alive."

"Can't it do the same thing if I let it out?"

"It can absolutely cause you pain. I won't deny that. But sometimes it's a little easier to let someone else help you carry the burden."

Joshua laughed bitterly. "I wouldn't wish this fucking load on my worst enemy." He wished he could just dump the whole damn thing. Problem was, it was his mind that was the fucking burden.

"Don't wish it on your enemy. Share it with someone who loves you. Because, Joshua?"

Joshua took a deep breath and summoned up the courage to meet Nash's gaze. "Yeah?"

"I do love you."

Joshua's mouth fell open, and he gawked at Nash. No one had ever told him they loved him before and he meant no one. Not his mother, his father—or a father figure—not a single person in his family or the families he'd lived with. He wasn't even sure he'd ever dreamed about someone saying those three words to him. Hearing Nash say them did funny things to Joshua's belly, but his head, his fucked-up mind didn't trust the words. So rather than deal with that fucking mess, he moved to one that made sense and surprisingly was less scary.

"Dr. Hobson and I were talking about my childhood. I don't like remembering, but he kept pushing me and pushing me. Made me so fucking mad that I started screaming at him when he said he understood. That was some major bullshit right there, because I asked him if he'd grown up with a crack whore for a mother. Or if he'd ever been rescued from one shit hole only to be thrown into another. You know what? He couldn't say he had, so I seriously fucking doubt he"—Joshua made the universal symbols for quotation marks with his fingers—"*understood*."

"And I take it you have?" Nash asked calmly.

"Hell yeah! That was the norm in my world. Looking back, I must ask myself if the protective service agencies do any screening of the foster parents. If they did, they did a really crappy job. Either that or they just didn't care. I mean, seriously, some of my foster moms were as bad as the bitch they took me from." Joshua pursed his lips, the injustice the state could inflict on a helpless kid was mind-blowingly wrong. "I don't know, but I'd think if they weren't going to help the kid, why even bother removing them from their home. Sure, their lives may suck, mine sure did, but at least it was a familiar suckiness. Removing them from a home, telling a kid they were there to help, that it was for their own good, that it would be better, only to drop them off with a sadistic crackhead was just fucking cruel."

"I've heard a lot of horror stories. I'm sorry you had to go through that."

"Don't pity me," Joshua spat. Nash's face fell, and Joshua instantly regretted his tone. "I'm sorry, but I hate that reaction almost as much as the situation."

"I don't pity you, Joshua. Yes, I feel bad that you, or anyone for that matter, would have to go through such a horrible ordeal. I'm also happy for anyone who has a good story to tell, and I have heard a few from people who grew up in foster care. I suppose it's like any parent, some are good and some just suck."

"You can say that again," Joshua agreed. "Anyway, that's what the conversation with the head shrink was about. He got me to talk about my past. It pissed me off, made me cry, then drained me. And quite honestly, Sir, I don't think I can go through it again this morning. Besides, you already know more than Dr. Hobson. You know the results."

"Do you mean the cutting?"

"Yeah."

"You haven't told Dr. Hobson?" Nash asked, sounding alarmed.

"He knows I used to cut myself, but I haven't gotten to the whole *exploring* thing yet. I'm sure that's on his list of to-dos with me."

"I've known him for a very long time," Nash explained. "I trust him, or I wouldn't have sent you to see him. Give it time. I know it has and will continue to help."

In Joshua's opinion, the jury was still out on whether therapy could help, but he wasn't about to get into it at the moment. Instead he nodded. His belly growled loudly, saving him from having to deal with any more memories. "All this talk has apparently worked up an appetite. How about you, Sir? You hungry yet?"

"Now that you mention it," Nash replied with a wink. "I'm not properly caffeinated yet either."

Joshua scrambled from the bed and grabbed Nash's mug, effectively ending any more conversation. He handed it to Nash. "Here, caffeinate, and I'll start breakfast."

Nash took the mug and smiled. "Thanks, I'll see you in the kitchen in a moment."

"Yes, Sir." Joshua bolted from the room before Nash could change his mind. Nash wouldn't drop that subject, that much Joshua was sure of. However, he'd take the reprieve, no matter how brief it might be.

JOSHUA EXITED the room, and only when his boy disappeared down the hall did Nash let out a long breath. He was glad Joshua had shared a little of his past with him. Joshua was like a sweet onion, multiple layers with each one hinting at what was beneath but unable to be fully appreciated until another was peeled away. He was learning about him and how to deal with the multifaceted gem that was Joshua. Nash had never dealt with someone so complex. Dealing with Joshua's issue was trial and error, like a shit-ton of error, but each little breakthrough was worth all the bad.

Nash finished his coffee, then grabbed the carafe and poured a second cup. Joshua was moving around the kitchen. Nash couldn't help but smile. He had no crazy notion that everything would suddenly be sunshine and rainbows. Still, he couldn't help but be giddy. Joshua was talking to him, trusting him with his secrets, and with each one revealed, they were getting stronger, closer. His cell phone beeped, and he retrieved it from the bedside table. He read the display and his smile grew even wider. His calendar notification reminded him it was Joshua's birthday tomorrow. He knew exactly what to get and how to celebrate. Surprisingly, it had nothing to do with sex. Although if everything went as well as Nash suspected it would, he'd have a warm, happy Joshua sharing his bed again tomorrow night.

Nash set his phone down, then threw off the covers. He slid from the bed, took another big gulp of his coffee, and started to set it on the tray, but then took another drink, and another. He refilled it again and headed out to join Joshua.

The scent of maple syrup and cinnamon greeted Nash. He moved up behind Joshua, who was standing at the stove, and looked over his shoulder. "Mmm, I love french toast."

Joshua turned his head and smiled. "Yeah, me too. I had a craving for something sweet."

"I always have a craving for something sweet," Nash replied. He pressed a soft kiss to Joshua's lips, then slid his mouth along Joshua's jaw to the sensitive spot beneath his ear. "Very sweet," he murmured before nipping and sucking Joshua's skin.

"I don't know. I think french toast may taste a little better. I'm sweaty and salty, not sweet."

"Are you arguing with me?" Nash asked against Joshua's neck.

"I wouldn't do that. Just disagreeing with your taste, Sir."

"We'll just have to agree to disagree on this one." Nash chuckled. He placed one last kiss to Joshua's neck, then reluctantly stepped back. Getting all touchy-feely while standing next to a hot stove wasn't the best of ideas. He turned and leaned against the counter, out of Joshua's way as he made breakfast and Nash finished another cup of coffee.

By the time the table was set and the plates heaping with french toast and ham, Nash was sufficiently caffeinated. He took a seat, laid his napkin in his lap, and picked up his fork.

"This looks and smells delicious." He took a bite, enjoying the sweet taste of maple, cinnamon, and powdered sugar. "Oh damn, it tastes even better!"

Joshua picked up his fork and smiled. "Better than me?"

"Close, but no," Nash assured him and then took another bite. Joshua didn't say another word. He just shook his head. Nash could tell by the expression on Joshua's face that he thought Nash was nuts. But that was okay. He was nuts—for Joshua.

"I have some work to catch up on this morning, so you'll have plenty of time to get your chores done," Nash informed him. "I was thinking this afternoon we'd work out in the yard. It's going to be a gorgeous day."

"Okay."

"Do you have any experience with gardening?"

"Not really, Sir. I can mow, rake, and the basics, but I don't really know much about plants."

"I don't have much of a green thumb either, so we have that in common too. Good thing everything in the yard is pretty much minimal maintenance. I wonder how hard it would be to try our hand with something simple, like a small herb garden."

"I don't know, Sir."

Nash took another bite of his breakfast. It really was quite good. He washed it down with a sip of orange juice before continuing. "Do you like to cook with fresh herbs?"

"Sure. They are way better than the dried and crushed variety you get out of a bottle."

"Cool, then I think it's worth a shot. Of course, it's completely self-serving. Better herbs means better meals for me," Nash said with a wide grin. "I'll look into what we'll need, but first"—He stabbed another big bite of french toast and held it up—"I'm going to finish this amazing breakfast."

Joshua was becoming quite proficient around the house, no doubt his chores becoming mindless, which left too much time for his mind to wander. Growing and maintaining a garden, in combination with the gift Nash intended on getting for Joshua, should keep his boy's hands and mind occupied. A couple of good things for Joshua to focus on during the day, keeping him happy. As time went on, Nash hoped Joshua's good thoughts would outweigh the bad ones every day.

Chapter Fifteen

THE CELEBRATION of Joshua's birth wasn't the only thing that had Nash excited, but he was eager about the gift. It wasn't only that he would be the one giving it to his boy. Nash had also been considering getting one for himself for years. He pulled into the lot of the local Humane Society and cut the engine.

Joshua was staring out the windshield with wide eyes at the building. "I thought you were taking me shopping?"

"I am."

"But this is a dog shelter."

"I'm quite aware of that. I remember you telling me you always wanted a dog but were never settled in one place long enough." Nash took Joshua's hand and brought it to his mouth, placing a soft kiss to Joshua's knuckles. "You're settled now. I figured this was the perfect place to add to our family by rescuing a pet who is without one."

Joshua continued to stare with an awestruck expression. Then suddenly he undid his seat belt and lunged at Nash. He wrapped his arms around Nash's neck and peppered him with kisses.

"You are the greatest human ever!"

Nash laughed at the onslaught of kisses. He'd known Joshua would be excited, but the sheer outpouring of joy from his boy made any reservations about sleepless nights and nightmares in potty training well worth any inconveniences.

"Okay, okay." Nash snorted. "How about we check and see if they even have a puppy you want first, huh?"

"Yes, Sir." Joshua kissed Nash one last time, then opened his door and stepped out.

Nash hurried to catch up. He wasn't even going to correct his boy for not walking at heel. This was Joshua's day, and he could do whatever he wanted—within reason—without repercussions. Nash opened the door and held it for Joshua.

The Humane Society was bustling with activity. Several men, women, and children crowded the various glass-walled rooms. The first had a sign over the entrance that read: Cat Castle. Nash avoided that room. He liked cats just fine but never had any interest in owning one. The thought of an animal shitting in his house for the entirety of its life as well as shredded curtains and furniture simply didn't appeal to him. Plus, given Nash's dominant nature, he couldn't see himself with a pet that refused to follow rules and always had to be the boss. That was his job. He would be the only alpha in his home. Period.

Nash steered Joshua to the room to their left called Puppy Palace. Several cages stacked two high lined the walls. In the center, a brightly painted concrete wall about thirty-six inches high split the room into six sections, each containing a puppy, all of various ages and breeds. He stopped next to one of the cages with a small black-and-white puppy with big floppy ears. The pup reached its paw out through the wire slots and barked.

"Well, aren't you just the cutest thing ever," Nash said. He shook the paw, then slid his fingers into the cage only to jerk them back when sharp puppy teeth clamped down on his flesh. "Ow! Naughty too. I like that." Nash chuckled. He looked over his shoulder toward Joshua. "How about this guy? He's cute."

Joshua came over, his gaze going to the puppy, then the card clipped to the cage. "It's a she, not a he, and she won't be cute and small for long. She'll be a beast. Probably close to a hundred pounds."

"Umm, yeah. That's a bit large."

Joshua walked away, studying each pup inside the cages. Nash followed him. "Do you have any idea what kind of dog you'd like?"

"I don't know. When I was real young, I always wanted one like Old Yeller. Then as I got a little older, I wanted one like Benji. You know, super smart but small enough to crawl up on my lap. Then…." Joshua shrugged and moved on.

Nash could tell by the way Joshua's voice trailed off and the sad tone in it, the good memories had morphed into bad. Probably the one where he gave up his dream of owning a dog. Nash didn't say anything further. He followed Joshua around the room as he carefully checked out the pups. He oohed and aahed over a couple, and he looked happy enough, but he never spent much time with any one of them, nor did he open a cage or ask for assistance.

A second pup grabbed Nash's attention. It was a furry-eared Dachshund that had big soulful eyes, and the best part, she licked Nash rather than bit, then rolled onto her back to show her belly. Nash briefly considered begging Joshua to pick the Dachshund but decided against it. This wasn't his day or gift; it was Joshua's. Plus, Nash didn't beg, but damn it was cute.

"Mind if we go check out the older dogs?"

"I don't mind at all," Nash said. "This is your day." He walked over to the door that read Doggy Dorm and held it open. "After you."

The Doggy Dorm was exponentially louder. The cages were larger as were the dogs. Some enclosures contained two or three dogs, all of whom seemed to be trying to bark over everyone else. There were hounds, boxers, German shepherds, pit bulls, big, big dogs with big, big voices, the sound echoing around the concrete room.

At the beginning of the next row, Joshua stopped outside of a cage and squatted down. His face lit up with excitement—the most reaction Nash had seen from Joshua since they'd entered the shelter.

"Hi, sweetie," Joshua murmured and held out his hand. The small reddish-brown dog with rosebud ears licked Joshua's fingers and whimpered.

Three cards were clipped to the cage and Nash studied the one with the picture of the dog Joshua was interested in. "It says her name is Hazel. She's a five-month-old terrier mix."

"Hazel," Joshua repeated, still petting the dog. "It fits her." Hazel went up on her back legs, rubbed her face against Joshua's hands, and continued to whimper. "I wonder if they will let me take her out of her cage."

"Hold on. I'll go find someone." Nash looked around until he spotted two young girls with *Volunteer* printed across the back of their shirts. He headed for them. They turned around when he approached, and the dark-haired girl's name tag read Missy. The blonde was Abi. "Hi, I was wondering if you could give us some information about one of the dogs."

"I'd love to," Missy said. "Which one are you interested in?"

"Hazel."

Missy smiled broadly. "Oh, she is such a sweetheart."

"You think we could take her out to the play yard?"

"Oh, for sure."

"I'll grab a leash," Abi offered.

Nash followed Missy to Hazel's cage. "Joshua, this is Missy. She can answer any questions for you."

Joshua stood, wiped his hand on his thigh, and waved.

"You have a good eye. Hazel is my favorite," Missy told Joshua and scratched Hazel's head through the chain link.

"Here ya go," Abi said, handing a leash to Missy.

Missy opened the cage door a crack and slipped the lead over Hazel's head. Once Hazel cleared the door, Missy closed it and handed the leash to Joshua. "You can spend as much time with her as you like, just don't let her off her leash or walk her around the other dogs."

"I won't."

Hazel was pulling against the leash, paws ineffectively scratching against the concrete floor.

Joshua laughed, followed Hazel, tossed his thanks over his shoulder, and was gone.

"Thank you," Nash told Missy.

"No problem. Just let me know when you're ready to put her back in her cage."

Nash went to join Joshua. He had a sneaking suspicion that Hazel wouldn't be going back into that cage.

OUT IN the play yard, Hazel jumped up on Joshua, her tail just a-wagging, then darted off before he could pet her. He led her to a covered area that had wooden benches set up. The moment he sat on one of the benches, Hazel jumped up next to him and put a paw on each of Joshua's shoulders. Joshua's heart melted. She was literally hugging him, making a small whimpering sound, and out of nowhere, Joshua began to cry. He wrapped his arms around the little dog and just bawled. He had no clue why, and the pup only made it worse when she started licking the tears away.

Jesus H. Christ, you're hopeless.

The emotional roller coaster he'd been on lately apparently wasn't going to stop at the gate anytime soon. He was a hot mess. Even though he didn't know the reason behind the outburst, he didn't try to hide the effect Hazel had on him when Nash sat next to him. Nash laid his hand on Joshua's lower back, caressing soothingly in a silent show of support. It felt right, as did the way his heart swelled with pure love for the pup in an instant. *This is what they must mean by love at first sight.*

"She's so damn sweet," Joshua sniffed.

"I think she has claimed you as her human."

Joshua lifted his head and met Nash's gaze. "You really think so? Do dogs really do that?"

"Yeah, they do, and yes, they can. Dogs have a great sense for people, and the way that one is hugging you, I'd say she's pretty happy she found you."

Joshua wiped his cheek on the top of Hazel's head. "I think there may be something wrong with her."

"What do you mean?"

"She's chosen a blubbering crybaby."

Nash slid his hand up Joshua's spine to his neck, gripped his hair, and tugged gently until Joshua looked at him. Nash pressed a quick kiss to Joshua's damp cheek. "She picked someone with a damn big heart. I don't know, but if I was you, I wouldn't talk bad about her human around her. Have you seen those teeth?"

Joshua turned his head and kissed Hazel's head again so Nash didn't see him roll his eyes. Silly man. It was so weird. Normally it pissed Joshua off to no end when he cried, no matter the reason. He had always associated tears with weakness, a belief pounded into him by one of his foster dads—literally. However, it didn't bother him that Hazel had made him cry. They were happy tears, dammit. He had a dog. *I own a dog!* Holy hell, if that wasn't enough to be emotional over, nothing was.

Hazel licked Joshua again, then hopped down off the bench. Joshua went to his feet and followed her as she sniffed around the yard. A man and woman brought out a large white Shepherd-type dog, but Hazel didn't seem interested in the newcomer. She seemed happy to walk around, looking back at Joshua every now and then. It was a strange feeling walking a dog, but one that wasn't unpleasant. After a while, Hazel rolled onto her back and rubbed it against the ground, cute puppy paws batting at the air. Joshua chuckled at her antics until she righted herself, ran at Joshua, and jumped up, tail wagging. Joshua bent to rub her back, and his laughter died in his throat when he was hit with a stench that made his eyes water.

"Oh damn, what the hell is that?" He smelled his hand and gagged. "Whoa, that's ripe."

Hazel seemed happy about her new scent, jumping on Joshua, spinning around in a circle, then jumping up again. Joshua couldn't stand it a second longer and went to his feet, waving his clean hand in front of his face. He scanned the yard, found Nash still sitting on the bench, and headed toward him.

"C'mon, Hazel, say hi to your other human." Joshua steered Hazel toward Nash.

Hazel complied easily, jumping right up onto Nash's lap.

"Hey, gi…." Nash's face contorted into an expression of utter disgust. Joshua couldn't help it. He burst out laughing.

"What the hell is that!" Nash said. He pushed Hazel off his lap.

"I don't know," Joshua got out between snorts of laughter. "She rolled in something."

Nash went to his feet and tried to get away from Hazel, who was suddenly very interested in getting up close and personal with Nash. Joshua laughed harder.

"No way is she getting in the car stinking like that," Nash insisted.

That had Joshua working to get his giggle fit under control. He couldn't imagine leaving Hazel at the Humane Society, but

Nash was right. They'd both be puking before they made it home surrounded by the stench.

"Maybe we can see if they will bathe her," Joshua suggested, hopeful.

"They're going to have to. C'mon, bring your mutt and keep her close to you," Nash demanded, hurrying away from Joshua and the stinky pup.

Luckily, Missy had no problem with arranging for Hazel to get a bath after she got a whiff of her. While Joshua and Nash waited for her return, they sat at a table with Abi. Joshua filled out the adoption papers while Nash went over Hazel's intake form.

"It says here she is untrainable," Nash pointed out.

"That's ridiculous," Joshua replied without looking up from the form. "How can a puppy be untrainable?"

"The previous owners were idiots," Abi remarked. "No dog is untrainable with a little work and patience."

"It also says aggressive and hyper," Nash added.

Joshua looked up just in time to see Abi roll her eyes. "Again, I say, the previous owners were idiots. Puppies are hyper. It's part of their charm, but she is most certainly not aggressive. If you ask me, they were making excuses on why they were bringing her back without taking any blame for their idiocy." Abi looked around to make sure no one was listening. "You didn't hear me say that," she said in a low voice, then winked.

Joshua winked back. Their loss was his gain. He'd seen such wisdom in Hazel's big brown eyes, and he swore he'd also seen pleading, like she was begging for a chance. She didn't have to beg. Joshua was prepared to work hard and be the best dog owner ever!

Thirty minutes later, Joshua was walking out with a freshly bathed Hazel, sporting a new pink collar and matching leash. Nash followed, his arms loaded down with a crate and a bag containing food, bowls, and toys. Joshua's belly flip-flopped with guilt at the expense. He hadn't expected Nash to spend so much on his birthday gift. Yet he wasn't about to let Hazel go, so he'd just have to figure out how make a little money of his own. He couldn't allow Nash to pay for everything Hazel would need going forward. Vet bills, food, grooming, and basic care would add up quickly. He'd figure it out, but today, he was going to enjoy his gift to the fullest.

Best birthday ever!

THE BREEZE from the ceiling fan cooled Nash's sweat-dampened skin, causing him to shiver. He grabbed the sheet, pulled it over them, and hugged Joshua close. A marathon session of lovemaking had left him sated and boneless. His boy had been extremely appreciative of his birthday gift and thanked Nash in a mind-blowing way. Not only had Joshua been enthusiastic, he'd actually initiated the sex, even getting a wee bit dominant. It was hot as hell. Not something Nash would tolerate on a regular basis, but as an occasional treat? Oh hell yeah!

Nash snuggled in farther and closed his eyes. Just as he started to doze off, Hazel began another round of barking and howling. "Ugh! She sure doesn't sleep very long."

"She's scared and lonely."

"Yes, well, she's going to have to get used to the crate. I'm not sharing my bed with a dog."

"I'm sorry, Sir. I'm sure she'll settle down soon," Joshua replied.

"I hope so."

Hazel had other plans. Her howling increased, and fifteen minutes later she was still at it. The longer she cried, the tenser Joshua became. It was no doubt killing his boy not to run to his baby girl. Hell, Nash wanted to rescue her. The pitiful sounds she made were shredding his heart, but he held fast and stayed where he was.

After a few more minutes, Joshua whispered, "Maybe I should go check on her."

Nash kissed Joshua's head, refusing to turn him loose. "If you give in to her, you'll be sending the wrong message."

"It's hard not to."

"I know." Nash kissed him again. "She has a warm bed, a full belly, and an empty bladder. I promise you, she's fine."

"Yes, Sir," Joshua said, but Nash heard the sadness in his tone.

Nash wasn't heartless. He did feel bad for the pup. Being in a new home with new sounds and smells was no doubt scary. However, he also knew if they gave in to her tonight, it would be all the easier for her to woo them again in the future. Nash was not having a dog in his bed. Having to sleep with one was an intimacy killer, and he wasn't having it. What they needed was a distraction from the woeful sounds.

Nash rolled Joshua onto his stomach and straddled him. "Let me help you with that tension." He laid his hands on Joshua's lower back, pressed down firmly, then moved up Joshua's back and down again. The muscles beneath his palms were hard with tension. He worked his fingers into the taut muscles, massaging each one until it yielded to his ministrations and Joshua began to relax beneath him. Hazel continued to cry but with less intensity and frequency.

"That feels good, Sir. Thank you."

"You're welcome, boy. You're doing the right thing by Hazel. A well-mannered pet is a benefit to the entire family. I remember when I was growing up, the kid who lived next door got a puppy. A golden retriever if I remember right. Anyway, that dog ran, barked, and bit. They thought it was so cute, but puppies grow up and before long it wasn't so cute anymore. About a year later, the dog and the kid were out playing and the dog clamped down on the kid's arm and wouldn't let go. I'm sure the dog was just playing as he'd always done, but this particular day caused some serious damage to the boy. The police got involved, and the dog had to be euthanized. Poor dog suffered a death sentence simply because he'd had the misfortune of having irresponsible owners."

"That's horrible. I'd never do that," Joshua insisted.

"I didn't say you would. I was making a point—an extreme one, I know. But the bottom line is, teaching puppies to follow rules and respect your status as pack leader will make for a happy and healthy dog."

"Mmm, I kind of like the notion of being a pack leader."

Nash stretched out on Joshua, grabbed the back of his hair, and tugged. "Don't get any ideas, boy. The pup is the only one you'll be leading. I'm the boss, period. Got it?"

Joshua grinned wryly. "I wouldn't have it any other way, Sir."

"Good answer." He kissed Joshua until they were both breathless, before rolling over to lie next to his boy. "Hear that?"

Joshua's brows stitched together. "I don't hear anything."

"Exactly. We won this round."

"Whatcha want to do to celebrate, Sir?" Joshua wiggled his ass, leaving no doubt as to how he wanted to celebrate.

Nash slapped his ass. "Simmer down, boy. I suggest we get some sleep while the princess is dozing. I seriously doubt the quiet will last for long, and you're still getting up in—" Nash glanced over at the digital clock on the side table. "—four and a half hours to get my coffee ready."

"Yes, Sir," Joshua said, actually looking a bit relieved.

Nash pulled him close once again and wrapped himself around his boy, taking in his warmth. "Night, boy."

"Good night, Sir." Joshua pressed a soft kiss to Nash's chest. "And thank you for the best birthday ever."

Nash's chest tightened. "You're welcome." He drifted off to sleep with a pleased feeling filling him and a smile on his face.

Chapter Sixteen

RAISING A puppy was a lot more work than Joshua could have imagined. Hazel was super smart and eager to please, but holy hell, was she a bundle of raw hyper craziness. If she wasn't chewing on the corner of the table, Joshua was chasing after her to rescue a shoe. One minute she was licking his face; the next trying to rip his fingers off. Outside to pee, inside, outside to poop, inside, outside to play, inside, outside to bark at a leaf, inside. In and out, in and out. Three days of rain meant dirty paws and numerous baths because puddles were just too tempting to resist running through. Still, Joshua wouldn't trade her for all the money in the world. Those moments when he finally got a second to relax from his chores and sit down for a moment, there was nothing more satisfying than doing it with a snuggly pup in his lap. Another satisfying event was watching Hazel and Nash fight for the title of alpha.

"Joshua!" Nash yelled from the other room.

The irritation in Nash's voice had Joshua dropping the towel he'd been using to dry dishes and rushing to Nash's office. "What has she done now?"

Nash sat back in his chair and pointed down. Joshua went around the desk to see Hazel trying to divest Nash of his sock. "She is having a difficult time with the rules. She simply doesn't respect my authority."

"Now you can't blame a girl for her fetishes, can you?"

"The hell I can't."

Nash sounded all growly, but he couldn't hide the slight curl of his lip or the fondness in his tone. He wasn't immune to Hazel's charm. Joshua lowered his head and swallowed down his laughter. He went to his knees, and Hazel instantly released her hold on Nash to rush to Joshua. She jumped in his lap, laid her paws on Joshua's shoulders, hugging him, and licked his ear.

"I was just finishing up the dishes. I'll take her out and let her run off some of this energy."

"I was about to take a break myself. I'll go with you."

"Awesome, let me grab her leash." He wished he could let Hazel run free. Eventually he'd be able to, but for now he simply didn't trust her. Normally she needed to be near either him or Nash, but out in the open…. Squirrel!

The ground was still damp from the rainy weather, but the sun was out and the temperatures were quickly moving toward the eighties. It was an absolutely beautiful day, and with Nash's hand in his and Hazel running around happily, it made it all the better. Joshua couldn't remember ever being this happy. Sure, panic and self-loathing tried to rear their ugly heads from time to time, but with how needy Hazel was and his adjustment to the added work, he would have little time to dwell on them.

He'd heard something about how a pet could heal a soul. He'd dismissed it as some silly made-up motivational quote. He no longer dismissed it. Hazel truly was helping him heal.

"You and Hazel want to walk down to the lake?"

"Yeah, I think she'd like that."

Nash bumped his shoulder against Joshua's. "Maybe do a little skinny dipping."

"I don't know, Sir. I'm thinking you and me getting naked might be too much of a distraction."

"Is that such a bad thing?"

"Only if we're not paying attention to a puppy who likes to play tug-of-war with anything she can get her mouth on. I don't know about you, but I'm not sure I trust her around certain exposed body parts."

Nash stumbled, the image Joshua had planted no doubt settling in. "Umm, yeah, I see your point. Let's get her worn out and get naked once she's in her crate."

"Good call, Sir. I'll be glad when I don't have to worry about her running off. I'll be able to trust her in the yard while I'm doing my chores."

"We could fence in part of the backyard behind the studio."

"That would be great, but you've already spent too much money." He'd train her soon enough. Hazel was extremely smart and learned quickly.

Nash squeezed Joshua's hand. "You forget, she's part of my family too. You both are, and if I can do something to make you two happy, then it makes me happy. So no arguments."

"Yes, Sir." Christ, he was a lucky man. He didn't know what he'd ever done to deserve someone like Nash. Nothing. It was a mistake, Joshua was sure. He'd done nothing to deserve Nash and…. He gave himself an internal shake and willed the ugly thoughts to go away. However, no matter how hard he tried, they lingered. A dark cloud on an otherwise beautiful day.

At the water's edge, Hazel tugged hard on the restraint, hell-bent on getting in the water.

"You should let her swim," Nash suggested.

Joshua hesitated, but Hazel kept tugging until he reluctantly removed her leash. She ran out as far as she could, swam a short distance, then headed back to shore. She spent the next half hour running wide open along the shore, kicking up a spray of water. Joshua couldn't help but smile at the pure joy Hazel was experiencing. The dark cloud receded.

NASH PUSHED open the door to the unused room at the back of his studio. He'd thought about turning it into a supply room or maybe even a small kitchen to save him trips to the main house when he was painting. Now he was glad the room had remained unused and unfinished. It would be the perfect space for Joshua. A hideaway, so to speak, that was his and his alone.

"I was thinking we should turn this into a little retreat for you. It would give you a place to come, shut the door, and block out the world when you want to be alone. We'd fence the back and put in a doggie door so Hazel can have access to the yard."

A strange whimper came from Joshua, and Nash turned around to find him clutching the doorframe, his body trembling and a look of distress on his face.

"Joshua?" Nash rushed to him and reached out to touch him, but Joshua jerked back, falling to his knees.

Alarm and concern filled Nash. *What the hell is going on?* He went to his knees before Joshua, whose eyes were open but glazed. Wherever his mind had gone, Nash wasn't part of the equation. Joshua wasn't looking at him.

"Joshua? What is it?"

Joshua continued to stare, unblinking. His trembling increased, and he wasn't breathing.

"Dammit, Joshua, breathe!" Nash grabbed Joshua's arms and shook him.

Nothing.

He pushed two fingers against the side of Joshua's neck, relieved when he felt the rapid but strong pulse. Nash took Joshua's face in both his hands. "C'mon, baby, breathe."

After what felt like an eternity, Joshua sucked in a harsh breath, and in the next second, tears streamed down his face and he sobbed.

Nash pulled him into a hug. "Are you in pain? Tell me where you hurt."

Joshua didn't respond, only buried his face in Nash's chest and sobbed. Nash had no clue what had triggered such an intense reaction. He didn't know what to say or do, so he simply held Joshua, rocking him gently, murmuring quiet, soothing words until the harsh sobs began to ease. Nash ran a gentle hand up and down Joshua's back, silently giving the distraught man what support he could while he cried.

After long moments, Joshua took a deep breath and then another. Without warning, Joshua tensed, then jerked back. His face contorted with rage and pain.

He angrily brushed away his tears. "I'm sorry, Sir. I don't… I…. Fuck!" He pounded his fist against the floor.

"Easy, don't hurt yourself," Nash said, keeping his voice calm. He took Joshua's hand in his and inspected Joshua's knuckles. They were an angry shade of red, but there didn't seem to be any abnormalities in the bones or broken skin. Keeping his hold on Joshua, Nash shifted and encouraged Joshua to sit next to him, their backs against the wall. Nash draped his arm over Joshua's shoulders and kept him close. "Do you want to talk about what just happened?"

Joshua took one more heavy breath, blew it out slowly, and then nodded. "I had a freak-out or flashback or whatever you want to call it. When Samuel left the house or when I got on his nerves, he'd lock me in a small bedroom."

"And this room reminds you of that room?"

Joshua lifted his head, looking around the room. He sniffed and then ran the back of his hand across his nose. He was still trembling but nowhere near as badly as he had been when Nash had first taken him into his arms.

"This one is much bigger. Samuel's room was only about eight by nine feet, and it didn't have a nice big window like yours. I think it's the stark white color of the walls and the fact there is nothing in here that triggered my meltdown. I…." Joshua swallowed hard. His brow furrowed as a play of emotions crossed his face. "Samuel locked me when he wanted to teach me a lesson. I… I didn't learn." Joshua hung his head and went silent.

Nash's first reaction was pure rage. Samuel, the same asshole who'd beaten Joshua to unconsciousness, then dumped him at a hospital and ran, needed to be brought up on charges for the things he'd forced Joshua to endure. But Nash pushed those feelings down. He still had a lot to learn about what this man had done to his boy, and the horrors slowly coming to light broke Nash's heart and caused his blood to boil. He'd deal with making sure Samuel got what was coming to him. But right now, Joshua was his priority. Nash wanted to pull him back into his arms and reassure Joshua he was safe and he'd never be locked up again. Joshua needed to work through his feelings, talk about them in order to begin healing. Joshua could only do that if he felt safe and trusted Nash. Nash didn't push, instead rested his hand on Joshua's thigh, letting him know he was there for him. At this point he thought it more important that Joshua hear himself rather than Nash, so he kept his words to a minimum, his tone as calm and matter-of-fact as possible.

"You're safe, and if you want to talk about it, I'm here to listen. If you're not ready, I'll simply hold you until you are."

"Thank you for that, Sir," Joshua said. He seemed to have better control over his emotions, his voice stronger when he continued. "I know in my head this isn't Samuel's room. He's not here, not my Dom anymore. Hasn't been for a long time. But my heart started racing like a freight train and I couldn't catch my breath. Completely irrational, I know that, but it didn't matter. There was no logic going on in my brain. It was like in that instant, I was transported there." Joshua curled his hands into fists so tightly his knuckles turned white. An angry glint flashed in his eyes, and he started trembling again.

Nash feared the stark room wasn't the place for Joshua to deal with these memories. Although Joshua was starting to trust Nash, it wasn't yet strong enough for Joshua to feel safe or have complete faith in Nash to keep him that way.

"Would you like to go snuggle up on the couch while we talk about this?" Nash offered.

"I'd like that, Sir."

Nash took Joshua's hand and gently uncurled his fist and entwined their fingers. Together they stood, and Nash led Joshua to the living room. Along the way, Nash grabbed a box of tissues and a bottle of water. He set the items on the coffee table, pulled a tissue from the box, and handed it to Joshua before he took a seat on the end of the couch.

He pulled Joshua half onto his lap. "Comfy?"

Joshua snuggled in. He laid his hand on Nash's stomach and drew random patterns with his fingers. "Yes, Sir. This is much better. Like I said, I know it was irrational, but even after we started talking about it, I was having a difficult time catching my breath in there. I kept getting flashes of Samuel's room."

"That's understandable," Nash said gently. "Are you ready to talk about it?" He hoped Joshua was willing to discuss the room and his reactions to it. Whether Joshua realized it yet or not, it was a good thing those dark ugly memories were seeing the light of day. Joshua would never be able to deal with them if he kept them suppressed and in turn would never heal.

"No, not really, but I suppose I need to," Joshua said quietly.

Nash swallowed down the relieved sigh. Thankfully, Joshua wasn't going to fall back on his normal tendency to avoid discussing his past.

When Joshua didn't say anything further, Nash squeezed him tight and gave voice to his thoughts. "I know it is scary bringing those past horrors into the present. However, I wholeheartedly believe talking about them will go a long way in helping you deal with them. Only then can you heal."

Joshua obviously took Nash's statement to heart because he blurted out, "I hated that goddamn room. At first, it would be for minutes, then hours. Once for over ten hours, with no food or drink while he was at work. I swear I thought my bladder was going to explode by the time he finally got home. I shouldn't have complained about it, because it only got worse after I did. He didn't stop locking me in there, but now hours turned into days. But hey, at least he left me a jug of water, scraps of food, and a bucket to relieve myself in. A big improvement, huh?"

Joshua was silent for a moment, but Nash didn't answer the question. There was no need, and Nash wasn't sure if Joshua had directed it at him anyway. Nash held him close and waited for Joshua to continue. He didn't have to wait long.

"Nights were the worst. There wasn't a single ray of light in that damn room. In the dark, my mind would wander and… I…." Joshua shook his head. "Honestly, it didn't matter if he locked me in there for thirty minutes or ten hours or three days. Leaving me alone with nothing to look at or do meant I was stuck with only the thoughts in my head, and trust me, that is one scary fucking place."

"I can see how that would be frightening, given your history of self-loathing. I wish someone in your past had had the good sense to help you with that, rather than exploiting it."

"You're helping me now."

"Yes, and you've come a long way." He placed a soft kiss to the top of Joshua's head. "I'm very proud of you."

"Thank you, Sir, but the credit really goes to you. I'm still as fucked-up as I've ever been. You are just much better at controlling me." He chuckled, but if he was going for light or happy, he wasn't terribly convincing.

Hmm. Nash wasn't quite sure how to take Joshua's statement. It worried him that Joshua felt he was "fucked-up." Nash had hoped that with all the progress they had made working together that Joshua would believe he was healthier both physically and mentally. Nash needed to work harder on convincing the man that he wasn't fucked-up because his self-image was much more important than what others thought.

Nash ran his hand up and down Joshua's arm in a soothing manner. "I've seen you sitting quietly without prompting. You are far less twitchy and much more peaceful, so I'm going to hope that your head is a little less scary nowadays."

"It's because I have something good to think about these days. Whenever I start thinking too much about what I can't do or my past, I just start focusing on you and ways to please you."

"That means a great deal to me. It means you're growing as my submissive, but that's only a part of who you are. You are so much more than that, and it's my job to convince you of that."

Chapter Seventeen

SINCE MEETING Joshua at the club all those months ago, Nash had run the gauntlet of emotions. The attraction toward the other man was off the charts, and sexually it skyrocketed. However, their relationship quickly became beyond just sex. Nash wasn't sure if Joshua had felt the deep emotional connection as early as Nash had, but Nash was sure Joshua felt it now. Joshua hadn't told Nash he loved him. Still, there was no doubt. They were meant to be together—a belief Nash felt in his soul as he found himself thinking about Joshua all the time. It made work a bit of a challenge, and he was sure the people in his life got tired of him talking about Joshua all the time. But he couldn't help it. He wouldn't apologize. Joshua consumed him day and night.

Nash walked back in the door after waving goodbye to Joshua and Denny, who were taking Hazel to the dog park. He noticed a missed call on his cell phone and picked it up to retrieve the voicemail.

"Hello, Nash, it's Cedric returning your call. I'll be home the rest of the day. Call me back."

Nash sighed in relief. He couldn't wait to talk to Cedric about Joshua. He needed help and welcomed a professional perspective. He picked up the phone and called Cedric.

"Hello?"

"Hi, Cedric, it's Nash. Sorry I missed your call."

"That's okay. How are you?"

"Fine." He walked to the window overlooking the backyard and leaned his forehead against the glass, having a hard time getting his scattered thoughts together so he could speak to Cedric.

"'Fine' is such generic word, Nash. How about you tell me how you really are."

"I mean… fine. Good…." He turned and leaned on the windowsill, facing the room. "Who am I kidding. I'm a fucking mess." Nash cringed at how pathetic he sounded.

"Do you want to talk about it?"

"Yes, but I'd rather do this in person. Do you mind if I come over? I have a lovely new red wine we can share while I pour out my heart."

"Absolutely, but you understand I can't discuss what Joshua has said in private."

"I know. Do you mind if I come now?"

"I don't mind at all. I look forward to seeing you, Nash," Cedric said softly, and Nash could hear the concern in his friend's tone.

"Great. See you soon." He hung up and turned once more to look out over the backyard. He took several deep breaths. His mind was still racing, his thoughts scattered, but hopefully Cedric would help him find some balance.

"THANKS FOR meeting me, Cedric."

"I rarely turn down a chance to see an old friend, especially one who brings wine." Cedric picked up his glass and raised it toward Nash before taking a sip. "How are things going?"

"Not bad, but I'm hoping you can help me make them a whole lot better."

"Like I told you on the phone, I can't discuss Joshua with you. You're my dear friend, but I will not break my oath to my profession."

"And I would hope you know I would never ask you to do that. It's me that I want to talk about."

Cedric raised a brow.

"Well, how best to deal with Joshua," Nash amended.

"We haven't really talked much about your contract."

"It's more than just the contract. I love him, and I want to do what's best for him."

"And you're not sure if you are?"

Nash ran his fingers through his hair. "When it comes to Joshua, I'm not sure of anything anymore."

"Except that you love him." Cedric leaned back and sipped his drink, then favored Nash with a small smile.

Nash nodded. "Yes, which makes this all the more difficult. I knew he was going to be a challenge. I was warned he didn't have limits, but I had confidence in myself. I knew I would never damage him. But now I'm not so sure." Nash leaned back and looked at the ceiling for a moment, thinking. "I'm worried my love for him is making it difficult to push him to deal with the hard things. He's struggling. I'm struggling. I want to help him so badly that it's all I think about."

"You're a good man, Nash. If anyone can help this boy, it's you. I know you're not sure at the moment, but the desire and passion to help him speaks volumes."

"I'm not sure if it will matter. He had a major breakdown yesterday and—"

Cedric sat upright, his features etched with alarm. "Is he okay? Why didn't you call me?"

"He's okay this morning," Nash assured him. "He and Denny took the new pup to the dog park."

"He got a dog? Wow, a lot has changed since I saw him last week."

"I'm sure he'll tell you about it tomorrow during your session with him, which is another reason I needed to see you today. Are you aware that Joshua was abused by a Dom?" Nash nearly choked on the word. "That's an insult to Dominants. This… This… sadistic fucker basically locked him in a small room with nothing but a pot to piss in for days. I'm sure you're aware of what happens to Joshua when he is left with his own thoughts for too long."

Cedric leaned back in his chair and anger flashed across his features, but he composed himself quickly. "I didn't know."

"I don't think either of us truly understands the full depth of the abuse and trauma Joshua has experienced. The past ten days have been extremely hard on him. The breakthrough he had with you at his last session and his breakdown yesterday have me questioning everything I do or say to him. My confidence is completely shaken."

"I'm sure I don't have to tell you that a Dominant without confidence in his abilities is not a good thing."

Nash bit at his bottom lip and nodded. Cedric, being a Dominant in a long-term relationship, understood Nash's concerns without having to go into depth. A Dom should never raise his hand, bind, or do anything to his submissive without complete confidence in his abilities. It was one thing to demand his submissive put his Dom's pleasure and needs before his own. It was never okay for that Dom to put those things above the needs of his boy.

"You do know that, right?" Cedric prompted.

"Of course I do," Nash barked, proof of just how worried he was. "Sorry, I'm just so goddamn frustrated. I do know I can't be what Joshua needs if I can't get a handle on this doubt. I also know that I will do anything to make sure he is healthy and happy. Anything!"

Cedric's smile was softer now. "I'm concerned about him as well, but the mere fact that you're here tells me he's safer with you than anyone, that you wouldn't ever intentionally cause him harm. But right now, it's you I'm concerned about. Tell me about your relationship with him."

"It's good... most of the time. He does well with chores and taking care of me. We've found some limits, although I suspect he's still trying to manipulate me." Nash looked at the table as the words came faster and the dam cracked. "We don't seem to have any structure. One minute, everything is going great, I think we're making progress, then *bam*, we hit a wall and stumble back two steps. Each wall we hit has me rethinking what I'm doing, and each tear he sheds rips out my fucking heart."

Nash took a sip of his wine, hating the way his hands were trembling and the quickness of his pulse. A deep breath and he continued: "Joshua was a mess after the last session with you. We really didn't talk about it. I held him a lot, told him he could talk to me about anything, but I didn't push. Instead, I let him ignore it. I did my best to make him happy so he wouldn't have to think about it because of what those damn tears do to me. The last week has been one orgasm after another at night, and to keep him from thinking too much during the day, I got him a goddamn dog!"

"The fact that you are aware of the issues gives me hope," Cedric said gently. "We, as Doms, are not expected to be perfect, right?"

"But I want to be perfect for him," Nash insisted. "I have to be, but I'm not pushing him. I'm letting him coast. I'm screwing up, Cedric, because I don't want to see him ache. I don't want to open up wounds and drag out the crap that he's got to deal with because it hurts me to see him hurt. I'm being unfair to him and perpetuating his lack of understanding about himself for purely selfish reasons, and it's just so damn frightening that I may mess him up even further." He took a deep breath and raised his eyes to meet Cedric's. "I cannot fail him, Cedric. I can't be just another in a long list of people who have taken from him and not given back."

"It's going to be difficult for both of you to push past it." Cedric set his glass down on the table without taking another sip. "I knew when you called me about setting up a meeting with your boy, that this was going to be hard for you. As Doms, it's not our way. We don't want to ask others to do for our boys what we can't. But sometimes, especially in the case of Joshua, that's exactly what has to be done. He has deep-seated issues that you cannot deal with on your own, no matter how much you love him. You did the right thing. You're doing the right thing. But it's going to take time, Nash. Some days it will be one step forward and two back, but you'll also have those days when you take two and only fall back one. We're dealing with decades of mistrust and abuse. That can't be overcome in a matter of days or weeks. It's going to take years."

"I know." Nash sighed and said it again. "I know." Unable to sit still any longer, Nash got up and began to pace. "But now what do I do? He needs structure; he needs pain; he needs consistency, but I don't know that I can give him those things. At least not in my current state of mind." He walked the length of the room as he spoke and then turned. "I don't want to neglect the things he needs. I truly believe he's a natural submissive. He wants it, wants to find joy in it. Which is really surprising, considering his past, but I can't seem to get him to where he takes real joy in it. Sexual release, yes, but not the rest."

"And he won't until he finds true peace within. Look, I'm skirting a fine line here, Nash. I'm trying to help without betraying my duty to Joshua. What I can tell you, since we discussed many of these things before Joshua became my patient, is he's allowed himself to be abused without knowing any better and spends huge amounts of emotional energy feeling like a failure, feeling like he isn't good enough. Those feelings have been validated over and over again by numerous people throughout his life."

Nash sat down, picked up his glass, and swirled the dark red liquid. It splashed around the rim before he set it back down, and he whispered, "I'm worried that I added to that list. I don't want to be one of many. I want to be the one whom he can trust."

Cedric nodded and frowned. "Sure. That's something to be concerned about, of course," he said finally. "It feels like a risk to you, and I know you. You don't like to take risks. But Nash, how are you helping him find that freedom and joy he craves, and frankly, that you do as well, by keeping him sheltered from the things that haunt him? They will only continue to do so. Joshua is, as you say, very smart. He'll figure out he's not being challenged the way he needs to be. You don't want him to come to you and say that either, do you?" Cedric picked up his drink again. "You're smart enough to know what happens when infection is left in a wound."

"I know all that." Nash frowned. "Intellectually, I know that. I understand it as more than theory. I know very well that those past abuses can't be left to fester. Of course I know, but I can't let it go. And until I can, I don't trust myself to do a scene with him. I can't risk it. But what does that mean for Joshua? What about his pain issues and his need to submit?" He growled in frustration. "I feel like I'm damned if I do and I'm fucked if I don't."

"Nash." Cedric looked at him thoughtfully. "I don't like to meddle in your relationship, but I have to admit I agree with you on this. I know the D/s role is very important to you both, but it's not as important as Joshua's mental health and well-being. It's very sad what has happened to him. But in my opinion, the most important thing you need to work on is getting him to trust you, which will be extremely difficult, if not nearly impossible, considering he's never had anyone in his life that he could trust."

"I know," Nash said sadly. He hated the fact he hadn't earned Joshua's trust. It was a blow to his ego even if he knew it wasn't completely his fault. It was still a hard pill to swallow. He found himself studying the top of the table as he tried to order his thoughts.

Cedric picked up his glass only to set it down again. "You don't have to go this alone. I know you care about him and want to meet all his needs, but Nash, this is bigger than you—this is about years of mental and physical abuse, and you simply don't have the tools or the knowledge to help him. But you knew that. That's why you asked me to help." He leaned across the table and tapped it, making sure Nash met his eyes. "You can't help him, but we can together. You can't do this on your own."

Nash didn't answer right away; he couldn't. He reached for his neglected wine and sipped it, trying to think calmly. It was far too easy to insist that of course he could do it on his own. Joshua was his responsibility, but Cedric was right; this was bigger than him. The trouble, he decided, was that the thought of Joshua brought up so many emotions at once that it was hard to identify them all and know what to do or how to react in any given moment. There were all the sexual feelings, some of which were becoming rather complex, and then the affection and admiration. The enjoyment of his conversation and his smile, of his teasing and his laughter. The sounds of him coming and begging. The tears. The discussion and Joshua finally facing the hard things. The scary things in the closet and under the bed. The willingness to bring them out, face them, and deal with them. To learn. To move on. To heal.

"I know," Nash finally admitted quietly, setting his glass down. "No matter how much I wish otherwise, I can't." His voice was rough, and he looked at Cedric with a small, weak smile. "I need you. I need to learn to ask for help."

Cedric reached across the table and patted Nash's forearm. "You have some very difficult and emotional struggles ahead of you. Both of you do. You have nightmares to get past. I'm here for you both."

"Thank you," Nash said roughly. "Now I just need to figure out what my next move should be. How can I satisfy his submissive needs as well as deal with his pain issues?" He thought for a moment, considering the continuation of at least morning discipline and bondage scenes only, but shook his head. "I'm not quite sure how to handle those things."

"Joshua craves physical pain so he doesn't have to deal with the pain in his heart. You can no longer facilitate that," he suggested. "However, that doesn't mean you have to completely change your approach. Joshua can still submit. He still needs help in keeping him grounded. It does him no good to dwell in the past all the time but bring his memories out, deal with them in small doses. Yes, he has to face them, but you can't overwhelm him either."

"So you're saying I should continue to keep him on task, expect him to do his chores, put me and my needs first the majority of the time. Find a balance. I get that, but I don't want to reward him for merely doing what I expect of him. I can no longer use discipline or punishment in the ways that I have, but he needs positive reinforcements, something to strive for. If it's not pain, what is it?"

"Save his favorite rewards for breakthroughs or for when he exceeds your expectations, and he'll work harder."

"I don't want to let him think I'm withdrawing anything—my affection or my respect." God, he was so confused. He felt like a rank beginner, totally out of his element. He was just lucky he had Malcolm and Cedric at his back.

"No, no, affection isn't a reward really. Sleeping in your bed, getting off, free time, those things are rewards. But of course I wouldn't change your style or your methods without discussing it with him, explaining that this is a new phase of your relationship. That you still care for him, respect him, love him, whatever terms you use."

Nash sighed. "Jesus. I can't remember the last time I've been this unsure of my abilities as a Dom."

"You have the potential to do two vastly divergent things to Joshua. You can help him, or you can harm him." Cedric's voice was soft. "Every time you open your mouth, every time you reward, scold, bind, blindfold, fuck, tease, kiss, ask, or order him, you are either helping him or harming him. If you're not doing one—you're doing the other. If you don't know that or you don't have faith in your abilities or allow self-doubt to cripple you, then I assure you, you will harm him."

"It's the last thing I want to do."

"Then you need to take a good long look in the mirror and ask yourself, can you be the man Joshua needs. If you can't answer yes with absolute conviction, then you know what you need to do."

The thought of giving up on Joshua made Nash physically sick to his stomach. He wanted Joshua more than anything. Nash shook his head. No, he wanted a happy and healthy Joshua more than anything. So, the real question Nash had to ask himself—was he strong enough?

Chapter Eighteen

SITTING ON the couch, feet propped up on the coffee table, Joshua ran his hand along Hazel's back. The soft fur against his palm had a calming effect on him. It amazed him how quickly the little pup had become such a comfort to him. Something he seriously needed at the moment, considering Nash was sitting tensely on the other side of him, picking at a hangnail on his thumb. After what had happened in the studio, Joshua wasn't surprised that Nash would want to talk about it, but to see the man so visibly upset and unsure, Joshua hadn't expected that.

Sure, he knew Nash sometimes struggled with what to do with him. After all, dealing with his fucked-up issues would stress anyone out. However, he hadn't seen Nash react quite this severely, and to be honest, it scared Joshua. He couldn't help but think the inevitable was about to happen. Eventually everyone got tired of having to deal with his issues, and honestly, he couldn't blame them. He'd sure had his fill of disappointment throughout his life, but losing Nash…. Bile rose up in his throat, and he struggled to push it back down. While he'd always hated moving around, he'd learned to deal with it by not allowing himself to get attached to any one place or person. This time would be different. This time would devastate him.

As if Nash was reading his mind, knew Joshua's greatest fear, he said, "We have some hard choices to make going forward, but I want you to know that one way or another, we will get through this. I won't give up on us."

The relief was so profound Joshua wanted to weep. He couldn't respond, his throat tight, and thankfully Nash didn't ask him to.

Instead, Nash laid his hand on Joshua's thigh, squeezed gently, and asked, "Would you mind if we put Hazel in her crate while we talk? I'd like to have your full attention, okay?"

"Yes, Sir. I'll be right back." He picked Hazel up and, on trembling legs, took her to the bedroom and gently placed her in her crate. She looked up at him with those sad eyes. "It's okay," he assured her and patted her head. "It's going to be okay." At least he hoped it would be. Nash telling him he wasn't going to give up on them gave him at least a glimmer of hope. Joshua closed the door and engaged the latch. Strangely, Hazel didn't cry or so much as whimper. She simply spun around twice on her bed and lay down. Maybe dogs could truly read people's emotions. If they could, it was no surprise that Hazel didn't want to stress him out any more than he already was. When he returned to the living room, the tension increased tenfold when he spotted their contract lying on the coffee table.

His mouth suddenly dry, he stopped at the entryway. "I'm going to get something to drink. Would you like something, Sir?"

"Water would be great, thank you."

Joshua went to the kitchen, chugged down an entire glass of water to soothe his sore throat, then prepared two glasses of ice water and took them to the living room. He set them on the coffee table, sat at the end of the couch, and pulled his feet up beneath him. He glanced back and forth from the contract to Nash but didn't ask about it.

Finally, after what felt like an eternity, Nash picked up the contract, a sad expression on his face. "I can no longer abide by this, as I no longer believe it's in the best interest for either of us," he said, holding up the contract. He threw it back on the table, and this time when he looked at Joshua, the sadness had been replaced with determination. "But I'm hoping we can draw up a new agreement we can both commit to."

"I'm good with whatever you decide, Sir," Joshua responded hesitantly.

"That's just it, Joshua. This can't be about me. It has to be about both of us." He snatched up the contract again and ripped it in half. Nash reached for him and Joshua jerked away. "Oh, babe, I'm not upset. I did that because I don't want you making these decisions while you're still under the mindset of being my submissive." Joshua frowned and apparently, Nash noticed because he added, "I still want that, believe me. But right now, the most important thing is that we come to an agreement while being equals. Do you know what I mean?"

Joshua thought about it for a moment. It had hurt his heart to see Nash tear up the contract that bound them together. In that second he'd felt like he'd been tossed overboard into a sea of unknown and he didn't know how to swim. Then Nash's words rushed back, *I won't give up on us.*

Joshua clung to them like a life raft. "I think so, Sir."

"I'm going to ask you a favor."

Joshua tilted his head. "A favor, Sir?"

"Yes, I want, or rather, I need for you to refer to me by my name. At least for this discussion."

"I don't—"

Nash held up his hand. "I know it's hard for you, and I understand. But I really need you to think of me not as your Dom but as your equal right now."

That was like asking him not to breathe. It felt strange to refer to Nash by his first name, but Joshua wanted to make him happy. Hell, he wanted to be happy. Plus, the thought of being Nash's equal appealed to Joshua.

"Okay, I will try," he said in agreement.

"Great! Before we start getting into particulars, I should tell you I saw Cedric today."

Joshua stiffened. Oh fuck! Would Dr. Hobson really reveal the things he'd said to him in confidence?

Nash must have realized he was edging toward panic mode because he quickly added, "We didn't discuss your sessions. Cedric would never do that. You can trust him, I promise. We talked about me and some of the difficulties I'm having."

Joshua only felt marginally better. While he was relieved that Dr. Hobson wasn't telling Nash the things they had discussed, Joshua still had little doubt that the difficulties Nash was having were his fault. He didn't voice it, simply hung his head and waited to see what Nash would say on the subject.

"My difficulties have a lot to with the fact that I've lost confidence in myself. I'm questioning everything I say or do when it comes to you."

It is your fault. Joshua's heart sank. "I'm sorry, I know I'm fucked-up and hard to deal with."

"Hey, no apologies. We all have issues, some deeper than others. The fact that you're seeking help, opening up, and dealing with your nightmarish past gives me hope…." Nash shook his head. "No, I know I can work through mine and become a better person. The kind of man you can lean on."

Joshua laughed bitterly. "Yeah, right. I'm dealing with them so well. I'm not just a train wreck; I'm driving the fucking train."

Nash shifted on the couch to face Joshua. He took his hand in his and entwined their fingers. "I know it's hard for you to see your progress, but I've seen it and I want to help you progress even further. In order to do that, I need help, and you have no idea how difficult that is to say that. But it's true. The only thing that matters to me is you. You've become my life, and I will do whatever it takes to make you happy."

Tears burned at the back of Joshua's eyes, but he blinked them away. With his free hand, he grabbed his water and took a sip to dislodge the lump of emotion in his throat. "I don't know what to say. I don't understand why you want to or why you're going through so much. I… I just don't understand."

"Because I love you," Nash said with conviction.

"You're crazy. You do realize that, don't you," Joshua said, trying to make light of the subject rather than allow it to get any deeper. He wasn't sure how to deal with it, so joking seemed appropriate.

"I do. Crazy about you." Nash released Joshua's hand and ran the tip of his fingers gently along Joshua's jaw. Joshua briefly thought maybe he'd succeeded, but Nash wasn't having it. "Look, I know you're probably tired of the constant change that's been forced upon you, but this change isn't being forced. I want you to have a part in this one, to make decisions on your own, ask questions, and figure out where you want to be, what your goals are for the long-term, not just about today or tomorrow, but twenty years from now."

Joshua had thought it would be a quiet evening cuddled on the couch with Hazel and Nash. He wasn't prepared for a deep conversation, didn't want to talk about depressing or hard shit. His head throbbed and his pulse kicked up as panic began to settle into him. Part of him knew he was being irrational. Nash wasn't saying anything bad, but it didn't matter. That small voice in his head screamed, and adrenaline surged through him, kicking up his fight-or-flight response, a coping mechanism he'd relied on most of his life. It took every bit of willpower he could muster to stop from running out of the room. He took several deep, slow breaths in through his nose and out through his mouth. It helped a little.

Nash seemed to know Joshua was struggling because he ran a gentle hand over Joshua's thigh, a small, knowing smile on his face. He didn't say anything further until Joshua was able to get himself under control again.

Nash's smile grew as if he was saying *good job* without using words. "I know neither of us would be completely happy without some aspect of our D/s relationship. It's part of who we are. I realize you need structure, need tasks to keep you and your mind occupied, and that won't change. However, those things can't be the main focus for either of us."

"I don't understand what you're saying."

"Let me try this another way. As your Dom, I'm expected to know what you need, and some things are easy. For instance, I know you need structure. I know you need something to keep your mind occupied and challenged. You need to serve and you're searching for peace. Other needs are more difficult, obscure even. Those are the things I'm struggling with, and until I know what they are, what will be the most beneficial to your mental and physical health, I can't keep going at it blindly. I have to stop second-guessing myself. Does that make more sense?"

"I think so." It really didn't. He wasn't really sure what Nash was saying but didn't want to sound like an idiot.

"I'll be right back." Nash rose to his feet and left the room.

Joshua ran his fingers over his beard, then brushed his hair from his sweat-dampened brow. His heart rate had returned to normal, but he was still feeling jittery. It seemed like every fucking time he turned around, there was something new to deal with, another rule, a new emotion, change, change, change. Before he could ponder it further, Nash returned with two pads of paper and a couple of pens. He handed one of each to Joshua before returning to his seat next to Joshua.

"What I want you to do is write a goal for tomorrow, one for next week, next month, next year, and the final one in ten years. I'll do the same," Nash instructed.

Joshua tapped his pen on the paper. "You don't want much, do you?"

"Aww, c'mon, babe. This isn't supposed to be hard. Just write the first thing that pops into your head, okay?"

Joshua shrugged. "This should be interesting," he mumbled lowly. He numbered the page from one to five. Considered the first one and started to laugh. "I don't think it's a good idea for me to write the first thing that pops into my head."

"Why is that?" Nash asked.

"My goal for tomorrow is to get Hazel to make it through one day without biting my toes."

Nash laughed as well. "Umm, yeah, that's not exactly what I meant. How about we keep this about your personal goals or our relationship."

"Okay, sure." Joshua considered number one. What did he want to happen tomorrow? *I don't want to have a panic attack.* He wrote it down, then turned his attention to the other four.

NASH SPENT a few minutes writing down his responses, taking his own advice and answering with the first thing that popped into his mind. Sure, some things might be silly or even appear trivial to some, but they were completely honest. A small snapshot of what he hoped for in the future. He studied the answers one more time….

1. Wake up with Joshua and a smile
2. Spend an entire day laughing
3. Have more good days than bad
4. Have Joshua's trust
5. Married and living happily ever after with Joshua

Satisfied with the answers, he set the pad facedown on the table. From the expression of concentration on Joshua's face, he was thoroughly thinking about his answers. Nash would rather Joshua not put so much thought into them. Writing down the first thing that popped into his head would truly be the most honest. Nash didn't say anything. Instead he picked up his glass and went to his feet. He stood by the window, looking out at the backyard while he sipped on the cool liquid, giving Joshua time to complete his list. With each tick of the clock, Nash's curiosity grew, but he didn't rush Joshua, simply waited.

Several minutes later, Joshua finally said, "I'm finished."

Nash turned around to find Joshua looking distraught. Christ, had he fucked up again? This was supposed to be an easy challenge, and instead he had his boy upset. He set his empty glass on the table, went to Joshua, pulled him into a hug, and kissed him gently.

"I'm sorry. I didn't mean to get you upset. I thought this little exercise would be fun."

"Ignore me. I can fuck up a day at the park," Joshua said, sounding totally dejected.

"You stop that!" Nash demanded. "We have got to work on this self-loathing issue you struggle with. You're smart, sexy, and have a huge heart, and I won't have you talking about the man I love like that." Nash pulled back slightly to meet Joshua's gaze. "Understood?"

"I…." Joshua started to say something, then clapped his mouth shut and nodded.

Nash swallowed down his sigh. Man, he had a lot of work to do in helping Joshua build his confidence. Nash released his hold on Joshua, picked up the pad, and handed it to him. Only then did he take Joshua's list and read it.

1. No panic attack

2. Make it through a week without being a crybaby

3. Make Nash proud

4. Still be Nash's submissive

5. Alive

Nash rubbed at the ache in his chest as he read Joshua's responses. They both gave him hope and broke his heart at the same time, especially the last one. That one word was a testament of how hard Joshua struggled with depression.

"Our answers are pretty different, huh?" Joshua asked.

"Yup, but we're different people, and I think we can merge them," Nash said, trying his best to keep his tone neutral. "Take the first one, you don't want a panic attack. I want to wake up with you and a smile. I'd say that's a good start to making your goal real."

Joshua shrugged.

Nash continued. "Number two works as well. You don't want to cry, and I want us to spend the entire day laughing. They totally go together. The only one I'm concerned about is number five. Is there a reason you wouldn't be here in ten years?"

"It's the only thing I could think of. I try not to make plans beyond today."

"But in all seriousness, Joshua, you don't have any plans to harm yourself, do you?"

Again, Joshua shrugged. "Not at the moment, but that can change on any given day."

"You know I'm not going to allow that to happen if I can help it. I need you to tell me when you have thoughts like that. Promise me."

Joshua bowed his head. "Okay."

Nash took Joshua's face in his hands and forced him to look at him. "I mean it, Joshua. Promise me and mean it."

"I said I would," Joshua snapped.

"Have you discussed this with Cedric?"

"He knows."

Nash wrapped Joshua into a tight embrace. "It would kill me if anything happened to you. There is nothing we can't get through together. You have me, Cedric, Malcolm, and Denny all in your corner. You're not alone in this, babe."

Joshua stayed stiff for long moments, then finally, after what felt like an eternity, hugged Nash back. He didn't say anything, but he didn't need to. Nash knew his boy was relieved. He could feel it in the way his body slumped, melted into Nash's body. They weren't out of the woods, Joshua had a lot to discover, uncover, and deal with, but Nash would be there next to him every step of the way.

~*~

I have a new contract. I didn't think I needed a new one, but apparently Nash did and of course he's the boss. I agreed to it, because quite honestly, what choice did I have? Plus, he made a good argument. Now as I sit writing this, I don't know if I made the right decision. I don't know if I can survive without the bone-deep pain my mind and body crave. He's assured me that we'll find other ways to take me out of my head. I want to trust him, I do, but bruises, welts, and cuts have become my friends. They've been with me since as early as I can remember. I rely on them, look forward to them with wonderment as a child looks forward to Christmas. Without pain, the high it brings, the thrill, existence seems boring.

And what if he's wrong?

What if he can't find other methods?

What will that mean for me? What will happen when the monsters locked inside my closet no longer get their sacrifice of blood?

I'm scared, yet hopeful.

It's a very odd sensation.

Chapter Nineteen

ITCHY. IT was the one word that came to mind for explaining how he was feeling. It had been a week since the new contract had been signed, and Joshua was having an extremely challenging time dealing. The first couple of days had been easy enough. They even checked off the first successful goal. Nash had woken the next day with a smile on his face and Joshua hadn't had a panic attack. Then a second milestone when Joshua hadn't cried like a baby. Even with the difficult session he'd had with Dr. Hobson, he'd stayed strong, worked through it, and really had been proud of himself. That hadn't been on the list, but it was another success considering he rarely ever felt proud of himself. The problem he was facing now was number three on the list—make Nash proud.

The new contract was making it all the more difficult. Joshua had agreed to the changes, but he hadn't realized how hard it would be. Nash still called the shots. He set Joshua's schedule, gave him specific chores he had to complete. Between those and his care for Hazel, it kept him busy most of the time. Still, he found his mind wandering at times, and since morning discipline and physical punishment were no longer doled out, he couldn't fall back on those sensations to focus on. Not only didn't he have them, but fuck how he missed the burn, the way a good flogging could send him soaring. Especially today. Hazel had seen the vet earlier. She was in great physical shape, but the stress of the visit as well as the injections had left her exhausted and she'd been sleeping since they had returned home. Now, with his chores done and nothing to do, he was… itchy.

I want you to come to me with any concern, no matter how big or small.

Nash's words came floating back to him, and he considered them for a moment. Maybe he could talk Nash into just one more session to get him over the hump. It was worth a shot. He found

Nash in his office and quietly went inside and kneeled next to Nash's desk chair. Nash continued to type on his computer for a moment longer, then ran his fingers through Joshua's hair.

"What is it, boy?"

"I was wondering if…. Well, you see, I…."

"Deep breath, then tell me what you need," Nash encouraged.

Joshua complied, taking a deep breath, holding it for a second, then letting it out slowly. "I'm itchy, Sir. It's like my skin is too tight. I was wondering if… you know, just today we could do a scene."

"Joshua," Nash said gently. "You know why that's not a good idea."

Of course he knew. Nash had said it over and over. Nash wasn't confident in his abilities, and until he was, there would be no bondage or spankings of any kind. When Joshua had agreed, he'd figured there was no way a man with Nash's reputation could not be confident for long. A few days tops.

"I know, Sir. But I need it. Not only is my skin prickling but my chest feels tight and everything is tense. If I could just find some relief. Something to take my mind off it, you know?" Joshua peeked up from below his lashes to see the look of concentration. *Please say yes, please say yes.*

"Where is Hazel?"

"She's sleeping, Sir."

Nash went to his feet. "All right, let's go down to the playroom."

Joshua jumped to his feet. Damn, if he'd known it would have been this easy to change Nash's mind, he'd have asked days ago. He had to hold his excitement in check to keep from racing past Nash. He was so ready to fly, to fucking soar right out of his head.

In the playroom, Nash walked to the cabinet. "Go to the center of the room and strip."

Joshua didn't hesitate. He whipped his shirt off as he moved, then shimmied out of his pants. He folded his clothes and set them aside, then went to his display position. His cock was already hard and straining upward in anticipation.

When Nash turned around, he had a smile on his face and a long narrow plug in one hand, a plain cock ring in the other. He grabbed a small cart with wheels, brought it over near Joshua, and laid out his supplies.

Nash pointedly lubed the plug. "I'm not going to restrain you. You'll have to depend on your own will. You are to tell me if you're close to coming."

"I understand, Sir. I'm to tell you if I am close," Joshua repeated.

"Good. Now, I rather suspect that a ring might be of some use," Nash said dryly, holding it up.

"That's very thoughtful of you, Sir." *Now if you'll just fucking hurry*. Damn, he couldn't wait to have that damn itch relieved.

Nash squeezed the base of Joshua's shaft and snapped the ring on. "There you go. That should hold you for a bit. Now, bend over, hands on your knees, and push that sweet ass out."

Joshua wasn't so sure how long the cock ring would hold back his orgasm. He was aching to feel Nash's leather. He went to the position Nash had instructed and waited.

Nash apparently wasn't in a hurry. He spent quite some time smoothing his fingers over the flesh of Joshua's back and ass. Nash dug his blunt fingers into the skin of Joshua's right asscheek, then bent down and bit the other cheek just enough for Joshua to feel a spark of pain.

"Oh God." Joshua bit his lip and shifted a bit. Nash ran his lips over the abused flesh, then slipped the tip of one finger into Joshua's asshole for a brief moment. "Oh my God," Joshua hissed as Nash's finger entered him, and he raised his ass to meet it. He was quickly disappointed when Nash moved away. He whimpered and turned his head to look over his shoulder, careful not to look directly at Nash but curious about what he was doing.

"Eyes front, boy," Nash ordered.

Joshua snapped his head back to face the wall. "I'm sorry, Sir."

"Pain can come in many forms. I know you miss your regular spankings, but we can find other ways to satisfy the need," Nash whispered. Without warning, he thrust the plug into Joshua.

Joshua gasped loudly at the sudden, none-too-gentle invasion. It took him a second to adjust, and then he blew out a heavy breath.

"What you need to focus on is your normal chores. They can give you a sense of place, of what you are. When you know in your heart that you are submitting, you can take joy in these things. My job is to see that your needs are met, all your needs, the pleasurable ones and the painful ones." Nash tugged the plug, then thrust in, seating it. Joshua arched his back. He dug his fingers into his knees to keep from going up on tiptoes.

"You have to start trusting that I know what's best for you," Nash continued.

Joshua didn't respond. He couldn't. Not with the way Nash jostled the plug, the friction on Joshua's prostate driving him nuts. "Damn, that feels good," he groaned. He squirmed and gasped as Nash unseated and reseated the plug over and over again. Joshua's breath was coming quicker, his cock throbbing mercilessly.

"Are you aching? Are you craving my cock, or is it this you want?" Nash tugged on the plug, dragging it out of Joshua's body, then back in fast and hard, pegging Joshua's gland.

"You. Oh fuck, you, Sir. You!" Joshua cried. His words morphed to a long, drawn-out moan as Nash continued to play with the plug.

"But you seem to be enjoying this so much," Nash said.

"Yes!" Joshua tried to explain, tried to speak, but his ability to form rational words was gone, his entire focus narrowed in on his ass.

Nash thrust the plug faster, stretching, rubbing, overwhelming Joshua with sensation. The assault went on and on until Joshua could feel his orgasm coiling in his belly. His dick twitched madly as a steady stream of precum oozed from the small slit.

"Please, Sir! More!" Joshua begged. He pushed his ass out and rocked into each thrust from the plug.

Then suddenly the plug and Nash were gone.

"No!"

"Breathe, boy."

Joshua tried, but he couldn't get a full lungful of air in. His ass spasmed, cock throbbed, and he wanted to come so fucking bad it hurt.

"Joshua! Deep breaths."

The authoritative snap in Nash's voice demanded Joshua's attention, and he couldn't ignore it even if he wanted to. He took in several deep breaths as he'd been instructed. After a few seconds, he was back under control. He still wanted to blow a nut, but at least he was no longer in any immediate danger of going against Nash's wishes.

NASH HAD every intention of plugging his boy with a larger plug and sending him out to do yard work. It would certainly give Joshua something to focus on other than the itch that had settled over him. However, Nash had gone too far. There was no way Joshua would be able to make it up the stairs with the plug hitting his prostate. He'd be coming before he made it to the top stair. Then again, that was the good thing about being the boss. It was his right to change his mind. Plus, nothing said he couldn't plug his boy after he came. They'd both win. Rather than grabbing the larger toy, Nash snatched up a condom packet and opened it. He undid his pants and released his aching cock.

Joshua had gone silent, but he was in almost constant motion, swaying, trembling, his hands grasping his knees so tightly his knuckles were white. His need was so great he couldn't be still. Nash wasted no time getting the condom and rolling it down the length of his erection. He then grasped his dick around the base and lined the head up against Joshua's hole. With one slow push, he was deep inside Joshua. His warm tight ass clamped down hard on Nash's cock.

"Is this what you wanted?" Nash asked, moving slowly in and out of Joshua.

"Yes, so good," Joshua moaned.

Nash grabbed Joshua's hips, holding him steady as he increased his movements until he was pounding into his boy rapidly. Joshua babbled incoherently, his entire body tense and thrumming. It wouldn't be long.

"Wait for me, baby. Hold on."

"I…." Joshua gasped, his head snapping back, and he held his breath.

Nash knew Joshua would do his best to follow Nash's orders, but he was only human. One, two, three more hard thrusts and Nash's balls drew up. He released Joshua's right hip and slid his hand over sweat-slicked skin to find the cock ring.

"Come for me," Nash demanded, then released the ring, letting it fall to the floor.

"Yes! Yes! Yes!" Joshua cried as he gave in to his release.

Nash grabbed Joshua's hip again and pounded into him until Joshua was spent. Only then did Nash let go of the reins on his control and filled the condom deep within his boy.

Joshua finally relaxed, panting, gulping for air. Still incoherent, but Nash made out some of the words like "Thank you" and "So good."

"My boy."

"Sir" came a quiet reply.

Joshua's voice sounded hoarse. Joshua was shaking, every muscle pushed to its limit. Nash forced himself to pull away and disposed of his condom. "Hands and knees, boy."

Joshua fell into position with a heavy thud.

Nash couldn't stop the smile that spread across his face. He hadn't planned on getting off, but now that he had, his mind was clear. He still had some work to finish, but he suspected the grin would be firmly in place while doing so, thanks to his boy. Oh, and his boy would be thinking of him long after he left the playroom. Nash picked up the larger plug and secured it in its holster. He stared at it briefly, his smile growing. Oh yeah, his boy would have plenty to focus on.

~*~

So many good things have been happening. It's been a full month since Nash and I signed our new contract, and it's going well. Like really well. Which surprises me. I still ache at times to feel the kiss of his leather. To feel it against my skin once more is something I am striving for. Nash isn't leaving me hanging. I have learned to ask for what I need. Actually, not really. It's still a work in progress. But when the itching gets unbearable, I know I can ask and he'll help me.

Not all his methods are, shall I say, fun. I fucking hate the cock cage. It does its job, but Christ, it's irritating like nothing else. For some reason, every time he puts it on, I pop a boner or at least try to. I sabotage myself each and every time. I'm not sure why. My body betrays my mind, I suppose. The plugs are cool and the edging is intense. He's even got me doing yoga and working out. I'm okay with the physical stuff, the yoga not so much. I'm not that coordinated, but, hey, trying to stay balanced in some of those strange poses does take a lot of concentration.

Dr. Hobson started me on an antidepressant med. The jury is still out on whether it's helping. I don't feel any different. I was super tired the first couple of days, but I don't know, I think it may be a waste of time and money. The sadness and agitation still linger within me. I don't focus as much on it, but I know it's there, lurking, waiting. Sometimes I start to think about all I've done and gone through—shit I still have to go through—and I get overwhelmed. The hopelessness grabs me in its viselike grip and I can't breathe. If it weren't for Nash bringing me back from the edge of despair, I don't know what I'd do. I shared this with Dr. Hobson, and he's asked me to give the meds time, that sometimes it takes a while to find the right medication, so we'll see. He and Nash are working really hard to help. I can't let them down, so I'll take the "happy" pills.

Speaking of happy, I can't help but wonder if Nash is. I mean he acts like he is. He's been helping me in the garden, loves hanging out with Hazel, who I may add is a total fucking traitor. She has begun sleeping next to him on the couch, seeks out his attention, and begs him to go outside. I guess I shouldn't be bitter. She and I obviously know our place and who's alpha.

Nash's happiness…. Right.

So, I'm trying to gauge it, and no matter how much he smiles or laughs, I know he misses our scenes. I mean, how can he not? I want to give him what he needs, but how can I do that if he's the one making the rules? How long can a Dom go without being Dommy? I think I'll talk to Dr. Hobson about it today.

I'm starting to think about tomorrow and the next day and the next. Goals and looking forward to the future is a new concept for me. I'm scared to dream, terrified to hope, and yet....

Here I am, writing in this stupid journal, getting up every day, putting one foot in front of the other, dealing with change, and cracking the door open a little on the past. Maybe I'm not a coward. Maybe, just maybe, I have a future to look forward to.

Chapter Twenty

"YOU'VE BEEN doing some sunbathing, I see. You look great," Dr. Hobson complimented. He gestured toward the couch.

Joshua took a seat. "Thanks. Actually I've been doing some gardening."

"I didn't know you were a gardener."

"I'm not," Joshua explained. "Nash thought it would be a good idea to grow my own herbs. I'm not sure how it's going to turn out, but I'm giving it a shot."

"That's great. It's always good to try new things. Cooper has quite the green thumb so if you need any tips, I'm sure he'd be happy to help."

Joshua cocked his head. "Cooper?"

"Yes, my boy. He's maintained our garden for years."

It was the first time Cedric had shared anything personal with him. It made Joshua smile. "Thanks. I'll be sure to take you up on your offer if I run into a problem."

"Be sure that you do. Cooper loves to talk horticulture." Dr. Hobson sat in the chair across from Joshua and picked up his pen and pad. "So other than planting and sunning, how's the new arrangement going?"

Dr. Hobson knew all about the new contract he and Nash had signed. He also knew how difficult it had been the past month, but things were getting a little easier each day. "I'm still struggling with the no discipline or punishment, but I have to admit, the way Nash deals with it has been quite creative." Joshua grinned and shifted in his seat, jostling the plug. It wasn't something they used all the time, but they found it helped him deal with his anxiety on session days.

"From the look on your face, I'm guessing you're truly enjoying Nash's creativity?"

"Yes, sir."

"This week was your third goal. How'd it go?" Dr. Hobson inquired.

"I think Nash may have achieved his, but I'm not so sure about mine."

Dr. Hobson stared at him for a moment, waiting for him to continue. Joshua wasn't sure what else to say so he looked away. "What was Nash's goal?"

"To have more good days than bad. I think we're getting there. I haven't had a panic attack in two weeks and not a single urge to cut myself in a while. To be honest I have to give the credit to Hazel and the garden. They are keeping me super busy."

"But you're still finding time to write in your journal?"

"Yes, sir."

Dr. Hobson nodded. "That's good. I want you to keep that up."

"How come you never ask me to bring it with me? I thought you would have asked by now. Aren't you curious to what's in it?"

"That's your personal diary. It's a platform for you to write down your thoughts. Writing them gets them out of your head and onto paper."

"I hate to be the one to inform you, but it doesn't work."

"What doesn't work?"

"Getting them out of my head. I'm not sure anything can do that."

Dr. Hobson wrote something on his pad, then looked back up. He might not want to read Joshua's diary, but Joshua would love to get a glimpse at what Doc wrote about him.

"I should probably clarify my meaning," Dr. Hobson said. "It gets them out of your head, not to purge them from you to be forever trapped on the page, but for you to look at and consider. Have you read your diary from the beginning lately?"

"No, I've never done that."

"Maybe you should," Dr. Hobson suggested. "You might be pleasantly surprised at how far you've come."

"I'll think about it," Joshua said noncommittally. The emotions those entries brought out in him were still too raw. The good days really were starting to outweigh the bad just as Nash had hoped. Maybe once he was more comfortable with the whole "deserving happiness" notion, he'd consider reading the journal. But not yet.

"Now back to your goals. What was your thirty-day goal?"

"To make Nash proud."

"And you're not sure you reached it?"

"Nope," Joshua said curtly.

"I would think that since Nash reached his—the good days being more prevalent—that alone would make him proud of you. I know I am very proud of you."

Joshua thought about it for a minute. He supposed Dr. Hobson had a point. "I guess maybe I did reach it in that sense, but I don't know about the success in being the kind of submissive Nash can be proud of. I feel like I'm the reason he lost his confidence, and that bothers me."

"Do you think he needs to raise a hand to you in order to be a good Dom?"

"I think so."

Dr. Hobson set his pad down, then leaned back in his chair and crossed one leg over the other. "I'm going to let you in on a little secret. There are more variations to the definition of Dominant than you can ever imagine. Some do it part-time, full-time, occasionally, or somewhere in between. There are also those who never raise a single welt or red mark. I personally know a Dom like that, and he is very well-respected within the lifestyle. My point is, there is no single act that defines a Dom. It's a state of mind, not any one thing he or she does. Nash's confidence in his abilities has not changed. What has is whether they are the best for you. Those feelings and opinions are going to change over time as the two of you continue to grow and learn. So trust me, whether he raises a hand or not, Nash is very much a Dom."

"I guess, but I still can't help but feel that I'm letting him down. He's always enjoyed the bondage and he's a master of implements. He enjoys those things, and because of me and my fucked-up issues, I'm denying him those pleasures."

"Nash cares more about you than any implement he has ever wielded, I assure you. Your well-being is the most important aspect to him, and I can't reiterate enough how great a Dom that makes him. Give it time, Joshua. I'm positive you two will find a healthy balance that you'll both find pleasure in."

Joshua hoped that was true. He had to hold on to it, because he simply couldn't handle another failure in his life. He couldn't lose Nash. "Thank you for saying that. It helps a lot."

"First you have to want to get better. You have to learn to deal with your problems, not for him but for yourself."

Joshua shook his head. "I can't. Not right now. I want to do it for him. I owe him that."

"Joshua, long-term—"

"I know." Joshua lifted his head and met Dr. Hobson's gaze with determination. "I will do it for me, honest, but right now pleasing him is more important. Knowing he's there gets me through my bad days. I've never had anyone care about me like he does, and I'm not going to fuck it up."

Dr. Hobson smiled gently. "Okay. We'll work on your self-priority later. Any more nightmares?"

"Nope, not in an entire month," Joshua admitted with true joy. "I'm sure it has a lot to do with the fact that I've been in Nash's bed the entire time. Something about having him next to me, somehow keeps them at bay."

"Have you told him?"

"No."

"You know, it's okay to compliment him on things or even discuss what's working and what's not. In fact, I think you should suggest a meeting with him, say once a week. A time and place where you can speak frankly, not as his submissive but his equal."

Wow, it was as if Dr. Hobson and Nash were on the same page. Nash had just recommended the same thing that very morning. "Have you been talking to him?" Joshua asked.

"No, why?"

"You sound just like him," Joshua said slyly.

Dr. Hobson laughed. "More proof of just how good Nash is."

THE SCENT of linseed oil, varnish, and paint wafted up from the workbench as Nash took care to clean each brush. Not that they were soiled, as he hadn't added a single stroke to the painting. Each time Joshua went to see Cedric, Nash found himself unable to stand the confining walls of the house or relax enough to walk around the grounds. Instead, as he always had whenever he found himself twisted up inside, Nash sought comfort in his art.

"Is that me?"

Nash spun around to find Joshua standing at the door, staring at the unfinished painting. He dropped his brushes and rushed to the painting, snatching up the drop cloth. "I didn't hear you come in. How was your appointment?"

Joshua took Nash's wrist and stopped him. "Is this how you see me?" he asked, sounding awestruck.

"It's not done, but yes."

Joshua ghosted his finger over the outline. "You're very talented."

"I have a great subject."

Joshua shook his head. "No, this is extraordinary. How long have you been working on it?"

"Since shortly after I first saw you." Nash pulled his hand free and covered the painting. He then took Joshua in his arms. "You didn't answer me. How was your appointment?"

"It was good." Joshua smiled and Nash believed him. The truth reached his eyes. "Dr. Hobson said I'm a work in progress, but I'm getting there."

Nash tightened his hold and returned the smile. "Yes, you are. We both are." He pressed a soft kiss to Joshua's lips. "And I can't wait to see how we turn out."

~*~

"What you get by achieving your goals is not as important as what you become by achieving your goals."

~Zig Ziglar

Epilogue

NASH RAN the soft leather through his fingers. He swallowed down the lump of emotion that lodged in his throat. A year of tears and laughter, sacrifice and reward, pleasure and pain. There were some days he wasn't sure if they'd ever make it to their next goal, so many changes along the way, some good, some bad. Trial and error. But here they were standing before their friends, stronger not for reaching their dream but because of the struggles it took to achieve it.

Nash cleared his throat. "Joshua, kneel before me." He was delighted that his voice had come out clear and even.

Joshua smiled, his joy at the promise of the collar evident on his face. He took a deep breath and went to his knees, facing Nash. Nash returned the smile and held the collar up—a narrow band of soft leather with an intricate design rising out of a lotus flower.

"Take a good look at it, boy. Once I place it around your neck, it won't come off again."

Joshua's eyes were wide as he reached forward and ran a finger along the leather. "It's beautiful."

"A lotus to represent a new beginning after going through difficult times, emerging from that struggle and becoming a symbol of strength."

Joshua turned the leather over and tilted his head so that he could read the inscription. "A warrior worthy of love," Joshua whispered. He looked up at Nash with tears in his eyes. "Thank you, Sir." His voice was tight. He handed the collar back to Nash, then clasped his hands behind his back.

"You are a warrior," Nash said. "You are worthy of love, and I am honored that you've given that love to me in return. This collar is a symbol of your submission to me. You are mine. I will work hard every day to remain worthy of your submission, trust, and love." Nash placed the collar around Joshua's neck and attached the small clasp. Nash's breath hitched to see it around his boy's neck. *My boy!* He struggled for a second to get the overwhelming emotions back under control before he could speak. "Stand," he said hoarsely.

Joshua rolled gracefully to his feet, and it was apparent by the expression on Joshua's face that Nash wasn't the only one dealing with powerful emotions. Nash brushed his finger over the collar, then placed his hand over Joshua's heart.

"I am so proud of you and so honored you're mine. I love you," he whispered into Joshua's ear.

"I love you too," Joshua mouthed, and Nash's chest swelled with pride.

Nash nodded, then turned Joshua to face their friends. "My submissive," Nash announced with pride.

"Nash and Joshua!" Malcolm shouted.

A heartfelt applause echoed around the room as well as cheers from Doms and subs alike. Nash gave Joshua a little nudge. "All right, boy. You better go give Denny a closer look before the poor boy pees himself."

"We can't have that, Sir." Joshua chuckled.

"Enjoy. I'll find you later." He leaned in and pressed a soft kiss to Joshua's lips, speaking against them. "I love you."

"I love you too."

Joshua rushed off to talk to Denny and Cooper, and Nash thought he'd never get tired of hearing those words from his boy. The words he never thought he would hear. Nash walked over to Malcolm, who pulled Nash into a hug. "Congratulations, my friend. It was a beautiful ceremony."

Nash patted Malcolm's back and stepped back. "Thank you. It looks good on him."

"And looks good on you too."

"What's that?" Nash asked absently, his attention on the interaction between Joshua and the other subs. Joshua's pride was evident even from across the room.

"Happiness," Malcolm clarified.

Nash turned back to face Malcolm and winked. "It feels good too."

Cedric joined them and offered his hand. "Congratulations, Nash. I'm extremely happy for both of you."

Nash shook Cedric's hand and grinned. "We couldn't have done it without you. I am forever in your debt, my friend."

Cedric waved a dismissive hand. "Nonsense. You two did all the hard work. I merely listened while you two worked through it."

"Just accept my thanks, will you?"

Cedric laughed, then nodded. Leave it to Cedric to be humble. He was a good man, and whether he wanted to take credit for it or not, he was a huge part of the reason why Nash and Joshua had made it to this day. Nash's gaze drifted once again to Joshua, who was talking animatedly with the other boys.

"He looks happy, Nash. You're a very lucky man."

"I know. I really am," Nash said softly.

Sammy, one of the new boys Malcolm had recently hired, arrived with a silver tray of flutes filled with champagne. Malcolm picked up two and handed one to Nash before raising his.

"A toast!" Malcolm announced. He waved Joshua over before he began. "Thank you all for coming to share this special night with Nash and Joshua. I know it means a great deal to both of them."

Joshua joined Nash. Nash wrapped his arm around Joshua's waist and pulled him in close to his side.

Malcolm turned his glass toward them. "Every collar ceremony we witness is something special, but yours is even more so. You've both worked extremely hard and overcome some huge obstacles. You never gave up. I have never seen two people work or love as hard as you. Continue to hold on to each other, support each other, respect each other and love each other, and I have no doubt you two together can overcome anything! To Nash and Joshua!"

A chorus of "To Nash and Joshua" went up around the room. Nash felt himself tearing up again and was thankful for the flute to hide it behind as he took a sip of the bubbly.

Nash spent the better part of an hour accepting congratulations and chatting with his friends and peers. However, his eye and his focus never strayed from Joshua for too long.

After dinner and another round of toasts, he and Joshua finally got a moment to themselves. He pulled Joshua to him and kissed him soundly. "You've made me so damn proud. I can't tell you how happy I am at this moment."

"I think I may have a clue, since I feel like I could burst. I don't know how I can ever thank you enough for the collar, for standing by me, for—" Joshua gave him a watery grin. "—just everything, Sir."

"You earned every bit of happiness," Nash said softly. He ran his finger over the collar. "Just as you've earned this. You honor me by wearing it."

"I doubted this would ever happen, Sir," Joshua told him. "And it wouldn't have if it weren't for you. I owe you my unconditional loyalty and trust."

"And I promise to do whatever I can to continue to deserve those gifts."

"I know you will."

"Okay, Okay, this is getting a bit mushy, boy." Nash laughed softly. "I think I'd rather take you home and show you exactly what this night has meant to me."

Joshua pushed in closer and pressed his lips to Nash's. "There is nowhere I'd rather be than home with you, Sir."

Nash kissed him deeply, then took him by the hand and snuck away from the crowd. Tonight was simply another milestone, albeit an extremely important one. But still, just one of many yet to come. He had no delusions that it would be clear sailing from there. They still had many hurdles to maneuver through. But they had each other, and Malcolm was right—they could conquer anything as long as they did it together. He'd found Joshua looking over into the abyss of loneliness and despair. So many had given up on him, tossed him aside as someone who didn't matter, wasn't worthy. But Nash had known in his core, that they'd only had to pull Joshua back from the edge, turn him around, and he'd lead them to happiness. Nash had been right. Joshua not only led him to happiness but along the way, he became the love of Nash's life.

SJD PETERSON, better known as Jo, is an Amazon bestselling and award winning author of gay romance. Her books have received starred reviews in *USA Today*.

Jo currently lives in Greenville, South Carolina, having had enough of the Michigan winters to last her a lifetime. She has no idea where she'll end up next but wherever she goes, it will be snow and ice-free.

If you want to know more about Jo or when her next book will come out, please visit her website at www.sjdpeterson.com.

Facebook: www.facebook.com/SJD.Peterson
Twitter: @SJDPeterson
Email: sjdpeterson@gmail.com

OVERRIDE

SJD PETERSON

An Underground Club Tale

Don't judge a book by its cover....

At over six feet, with a body honed in the gym, auto worker Donavan Gregory is used to people assuming he's a dominant top. Unfortunately, they're wrong, and Donavan's desire to explore his submissive side goes unfulfilled.

Smaller and older than Donavan, Dr. Seth Manning might not look like a typical Dominant, but when the two men meet at Pride, Donavan realizes Seth might be his perfect counterpart. The trouble is, Donavan doesn't have as much experience with the BDSM world as he'd like. What could an educated, handsome, and confident man like Seth possibly see in someone like him? Seth must convince him that despite the differences on the surface, when it comes to kinky fun and discovery, they'll fit together just fine.

www.dreamspinnerpress.com

LIMITLESS
SJD PETERSON

An Underground Club Tale

Even within the context of the Underground BDSM Club, Joshua's desires are dark and extreme. Hopelessly addicted to pain and the high it gives him, he has no limits. Joshua would quite literally rather die than use a safeword, and he accepts that might be his fate. As much as he depends on others, he has yet to find a man who can gain his trust, and he has little hope that he ever will.

For Nash, acquiring Joshua from another Dom at the club is only the first step in what will be a long and arduous road to lure the young man back from the brink of self-destruction. He must do the impossible and win Joshua's trust, and he must be the one to set limits in their exploration—something he's unaccustomed to as a Dom. But Nash knows dominance doesn't always mean pushing a submissive's boundaries. It's about establishing a bond and fulfilling another man's needs. In Joshua's case, he'll have to strike a balance between meeting the young man's expectations and drawing firm lines that will save Joshua from himself.

www.dreamspinnerpress.com

GOING
OFF GRID
SJD PETERSON

Clay and Elliott are working toward a dream—working sixty-hour weeks for one of the oil companies that recently sprung up in North Dakota. The pay is good, but is it a fair trade for never seeing each other? The point becomes moot when the company folds, like so many others, and the couple is left with a difficult choice.

Should they find comparable work somewhere else, or is it time to throw caution to the wind and go after their goal—years earlier than they intended?

What they've always wanted is to be together and have time to enjoy it, so they follow their hearts. They're going off the grid and fixing up an old cabin so they can be self-sufficient. But when they go from all the conveniences of the modern world to outhouses, solar power, a shoestring budget, and more mosquitos than they ever thought possible, will they find there's such a thing as too much time together?

www.dreamspinnerpress.com

Remember When

SJD PETERSON

Life is simple and hopeful in youth. Luke and Nelson are best friends exploring their budding sexuality. They have big plans for the future, and nothing can stand in their way or tear them apart—except a family move that puts a continent between them.

Ten years later Luke and Nelson meet again, but nothing is simple anymore. As strong as the attraction remains, obligations and expectations come between them as Luke is forced to honor family responsibilities over the desires of his heart.

Impossibly fate sees fit to offer them a last opportunity to see what might have been. Will the third time be the charm, or is trust so badly broken it is impossible to repair? Can they recapture the innocent love they once knew and make up for all the wasted years? In a love story that spans half a lifetime, two friends destined for each other will have to fight hard for their happily ever after.

www.dreamspinnerpress.com

Roger

SJD PETERSON

Texas native Colt Burrow isn't happy about his third cold, lonely Christmas in frozen Michigan. But when fate sends him a gift in the form of an abandoned puppy, he can't keep his heart from melting. With the puppy's companionship, he doesn't feel so isolated anymore, and the holidays don't seem as bleak. He even finds enough Christmas spirit to take Roger tree shopping. But just when Colt's starting to hope Roger's owner doesn't show up… he does, and Colt doesn't want to say goodbye.

Will Roger end up being Colt's Christmas heartbreak… or his Christmas miracle?

www.dreamspinnerpress.com

Romance Redefined

SJD Peterson

Opposites attract, but are some differences too drastic for a romance to survive?

On the surface, Benson Howard Winthrop III and Hugh Bayard have a lot in common: they're young, handsome, and blessed to be one of the wealthiest couples in the country. Surely they have everything anyone could want. But Ben is no longer satisfied with their long-running relationship. Hugh's need to control every situation is suffocating him, and Ben needs to know if he can make it on his own merits by following his passion.

But Ben's mother isn't about to let her son live in a rundown apartment as a struggling actor. She's determined to get him back to his rightful place at the top of the social ladder—and back with Hugh.

Rekindling their romance will require more than doing what's expected. Ben and Hugh need to understand and embrace each other's differences. They'll have to support each other even when one makes a decision the other doesn't agree with. For their passionate love to grow, they will need to redefine the meaning of romance… only then can they find true happiness.

www.dreamspinnerpress.com

Something's
Brewing
at Joe's

SJD PETERSON

The promise of a dream job lures Murphy to Tampa, but he arrives to the rude awakening that the offer is on hold. Now he's got two choices: slink back to Michigan with his tail between his legs or stay and look for work. Things perk up when he goes into a coffee shop and learns the owner is looking for someone to renovate the apartment above it. He happily takes the job, only later realizing he's met Joe Sterling, Kaffeinate's proprietor, before… when they hooked up at a club Murphy's first night in Tampa.

Murphy and Joe are both proud, passionate, and outspoken. Neither is looking for a relationship, though they can't deny they go together as well as coffee and doughnuts, in spite of their tempers. But that's before Joe learns Murphy will be working for the corporation he believes is harming local businesses and the environment—and if Murphy will be supporting it, Joe wants nothing to do with him, dooming any possibility of an unexpected happy ending.

www.dreamspinnerpress.com

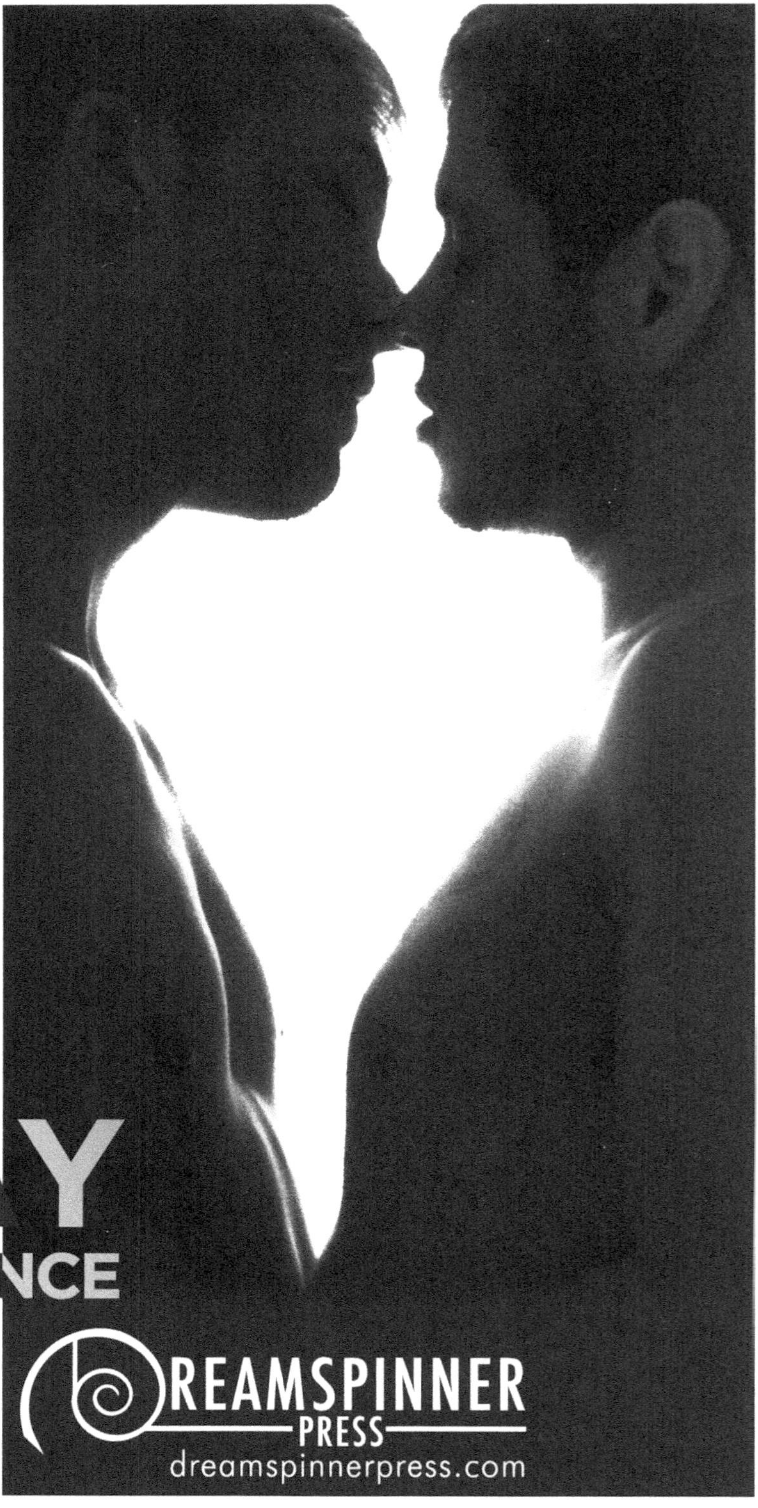

www.ingramcontent.com/pod-product-compliance
Lightning Source LLC
Chambersburg PA
CBHW060102260626
47160CB00005B/1768